AF797706

His Rules

Love that breaks all the rules.

Simran Betageri

pencil

ISBN 978-93-5458-232-5
© Simran Betageri 2021
Published in India 2021 by Pencil

A brand of
One Point Six Technologies Pvt. Ltd.
123, Building J2, Shram Seva Premises,
Wadala Truck Terminal, Wadala (E)
Mumbai 400037, Maharashtra, INDIA
E connect@thepencilapp.com
W www.thepencilapp.com

All rights reserved worldwide

No part of this publication may be reproduced, stored in or introduced into a retrieval system, or transmitted, in any form, or by any means (electronic, mechanical, photocopying, recording or otherwise), without the prior written permission of the Publisher. Any person who commits an unauthorized act in relation to this publication can be liable to criminal prosecution and civil claims for damages.

DISCLAIMER: *The opinions expressed in this book are those of the authors and do not purport to reflect the views of the Publisher.*

Author biography

"His Rules" is one of my best works, I wouldn't be able to finish this book if it weren't for my motivation to move forward. Most of my works are inspired by my real life but with a twist, as a post graduation student we hardly find time for ourselves but my passion to proceed with my stories pushes me to make time for my ambission, my goal in life is to travle around the world broadcasting my work to the whole wide world.

CONTENTS

Contract

Erika P.O.V

"Ma'am, it's time," my secretary informs me and I glance at the wall clock in my office, huh! It's almost 9 pm. time runs faster when you love what you do.
I smile at Sarah "You can go ahead, I will lock up when I'm done" I smile at her and she gives me a worried look, I know that look. she has been giving me that look for almost four years now.
Sarah is in her late forties with blonde hair, blue eyes, and a friendly smile always plastered on her face, maybe not right now but it always there
I smile at her again "I'll leave in 10, I promise" she smiles back but still worried, but leaves nonetheless. I sigh and get back to my work it's hard, working for an IT company also as the General manager but I've worked hard for this position and it's worth it.
I pack up in 10 minutes as promised and lock my room. I walk down the hallway to the elevator and press 0 at the parking lot. I walk to my black Auston martini and drive off to my house or OUR house I sigh and park in our driveway but find it empty. it's not a surprise that I'm home alone and I know it's been like this for four years but it still hurts, it didn't in the beginning but now it does.
grabbing my bag from my car I get out, I press my forefinger

at the scanner and open the door, being the IT person has its perks, I've installed all the high-tech technology in my house.
I walk inside the dead silent two-story house, I don't have maids because we are seldom home, I change into comfy cotton shorts and one of Dimitri's shirts and walk into the kitchen to make myself dinner. who is Dimitri, you ask?
Dimitri is my husband, been like that for almost four and a half years, it doesn't matter though cause it's gonna very end soon.
I glance at my bag and give it a long sad and longing look, I didn't mean for it to end like this but this is how it's supposed to be. it's almost five years and our time is up.
I shake my head to rid of these thoughts and concentrate on making dinner. I continue to cut, boil and fry vegetables and chicken until it's medium cooked. I have my dinner in silence and put the dirty dish in the dishwasher, cracking my stiff neck a little I walk back into my bedroom for some much-needed sleep, its the biggest room in the house with an attached bathroom, a walk-in wardrobe, dressing table, double couch, coffee table and a double bed with beautiful side tables.
I should feel great with all this luxury but I don't, it doesn't matter how much these costs but money alone is never enough, it wouldn't hurt so much if it were just me but being married and alone is kind of sad and depressing. I know I don't have the right to complain since I agreed to this but no matter how many times I console myself I just can't seem to get rid of these feelings.
As expected sleep didn't come to me that easily no matter how much I try to just blank out, I just can't. I keep glancing at the clock on the side table and it reads 2:30 am and he is

still not home, he should have been here, he is not even in another country constantly try, he was home but still not here. this always makes me think of the first time I did this, waiting for him I mean. it will always feel like that.

sometimes I wonder why I even agree to such a thing but then I think of my lovely family, their smiling faces make me forget that I live like this. it's worth it though, the deal with the devil, it's worth it but I wish I had just stuck to the contract as he did, not fall for his charm, not think of his whereabouts, not wait for him at the dinner table, not feel so stupid for feeling this way, sometimes I curse myself to feel like this, and what I hate the most about myself is that I have fallen in love with him.

Maybe it's the Idea of him, or that no that matter how rude or mean he is towards me we share the same reason for our marriage.
He did it for his family and I did it for mine, but the difference is that I let my emotions get involved and that is something he didn't let happen. He stayed true to the contract and I feel like an idiot for not doing the same.

I woke up with the sudden vibration of my phone, I opened my left eye and looked at my phone it was an unknown number, I glanced at the time and it was 3:45 am which meant that I had only slept for almost an hour. my phone kept buzzing in my hand and I finally swiped right.
"Hello?" I asked still half asleep.
"Erika," said a husky voice, a voice that I'm very aware of, I sat up
"Oliver?" I asked looking at my phone again but this was

not his number "whose number is this? and why are you calling me at this time?" I asked getting out of bed and slipping into my fluffy slippers.
"ahm.." he dragged " Can you pick me up?" he asked I could hear his nervousness.
"sure, where are you? are you ok?" I asked grabbing a jacket along the way towards the front door
"I... I'm at the police station," he said and I stopped on my track, and just stayed silent not expecting that.
"What?!" I yelled, "why are you there?" I asked looking for my wallet
"long story, just get here fast and also get some cash" with that he hung up.
I looked at my phone in frustration and went back to my room and grabbed some cash from the safe, I was out within minutes and drove to the nearest police station
I walked up to the reception and smile, the man at the reception looked at me weird and looked at me once over he would look at me strangely because I was in pink cotton shorts and Dimitri's shirt and a long knee-length coat, I smiled at him again and asked for Oliver Price
he smirked and asked me to just go inside, shrugging I went in and there was barely anyone in there, just a couple of cops and three deadly looking people, and Oliver.
inside the holding cell, he was badly beaten up. he had fresh blue and green bruising on his right eye and torn lip, bleeding forehead which he had a kerchief holding up. I cringed looking at his appearance. without any bruising, he was a very good-looking guy with blonde hair, green eyes, fair complexion, and a height of about 6ft.
I walked up to an officer " Hi, I'm here for him" I said pointing at Oliver who looked at me gratefully. the police

officer in his mid-thirties gave me a once over in a very creepy way', I should have worn better clothes' i think to myself

"I can't let him go just like that," he said smiling creepily "he was charged with assault on a decent man," he said and Oliver yelled from his cell

"That creep is not decent" he yelled punching at the bars "he hit me first and called me fag" he yelled making me snap my head towards him

"who did?" I asked now looking at Oliver and he nodded at a man sitting on the far end on a side table, he was badly bruised, he was an ugly-looking pothead.

"It was bound to happen you wouldn't have shown your ugly homo face to me, you deserve to burn in hell for going against nature" the pothead sneered at Oliver tugging at his handcuffs.

with that said I marched up at him and punched him straight in the face, the crunch was heard letting me know that I successfully broke his nose, I hit him again and knee in the balls also swamped om his leg

five minutes later I find myself sitting beside Oliver in his cell.

"I thought I asked you to bail me out," he said hiding his smile

I shrugged "me too" with that both of us started laughing.

"What do we do now?" he asked me and I shrugged not having a plan.

"I don't know, wait till morning I guess" he huffed but sobered up and looked at me pleading, I raised my eyebrow at him

"There is still a way" he looked at me hinting at something

I shook my head realizing what he was hinting at "nope, no

and no" I said looking away from him.
"Come on, please. I don't want to stay here any longer and this cop is starting to get on my nerve with the way he keeps looking at you" he purposely said loudly looking at the creepy cop.
I sighed and understood his point. I didn't like the way he was looking at me either, looks like we didn't have a choice.
I stood up holding the bars of the cell and called the cop "Can I make a phone call?" he looked at me for a minute but nodded anyway. he walked up to the cell and opened the gate.
"One phone call" he warned and I nodded, picking the receiver of the landline phone, I dialed the number which I have barely used in a long time. I didn't even know if he was going to answer, hoping for the best I waited as the line kept ringing.
I almost gave up when he didn't pick up but he did at the last moment
"Hello?" he asked in a deep husky voice, he was asleep I guess
"Dimitri," I said his name and he instantly sobered up.
"Erika?" he asked I could hear shuffling in the background and didn't think anything
"Yeah, I need a favor," I said glancing at the cop who was staring at me annoyed.
"What happened?" he asked shocked since I rarely ask for anything from him
"I'm at the High Line police station" I whispered knowing he was going to burst out
"What?" he yelled " Are you ok? did something happen," he asked I could hear him rushing in the background?
"it's not something bad, I just need you to bail us out," I said

hoping he would stop questioning and hurry the hell up. "I got to go" that I hung up
"Is he coming?" Oliver asked as soon as I was inside the cell again,
I look at him nodding "You know what this means right?" I asked "you need to come out to him" he grimly nodded at me but didn't say anything else
we didn't have to wait too long since Dimitri was here within 10 minutes 'he must have been nearby' i thought 'but why didn't he come home?' i was itching to ask him that but didn't
he strode in like he owned the place, something about him will always be a mystery, his dark hair was messed up maybe by running his hand in it, his hypnotizing grey eyes looked furious and his strong sharp jaw was clenched, his broad shoulders were stiff and his muscular body shook in anger.
I looked at Oliver who didn't look very much affected by him but there was still some nervousness.
I looked at the devil again and saw him staring right back at me with anger, he kept glancing between Oliver and me, and something flashed in his eyes.
the creepy cop cleared his throat to get Dimitri's attention but almost flinched with the way Dimitri looked at him.
this is going to be a long night...
The tension in the car was so thick that it can be cut with a knife, I sat silently in the passenger seat of Dimitri's Audi whereas Oliver sat quietly in the back, none of us tried to make a conversation.
long story short, Dimitri bailed us out. he threw bundles of cash on the cop's table who eagerly snatched it while grinning happily, 'good for him'
"What the hell were you thinking?" was the first thing that

came out of Dimitri's mouth after almost 10 minutes of excruciating silence
"I'm sorry, it's my fault" Oliver apologized grimly, wincing while he did so.
"Damn right, you are" he gripped the steering wheel "and what the hell are you wearing?" he asked me in a booming voice, I jumped in my seat.
"I rushed out as soon as I got his call," avoiding eye contact, pulling the coat closer to my body.
"I don't care what you do together at least don't screw up like this" was all he said before he pulled into our driveway, he smalled the door on his way out and marched towards the front door.
I glanced back at Oliver who was looking at Dimitri's figure until he disappeared behind the door, he then looked at me with wide eyes.
"What the hell? did he assume we were going behind his back" he yelled in disbelieve, I shook my head and followed behind Dimitri
he was in the kitchen leaning in front of the refrigerator "it's not what you think" I said but he ignored me like always but I continued "we were not together when he was arrested "I said hoping he would at least look at me
he snorted when the words left my mouth "right" he said pulling a beer bottle out of the fridge. "so, you just magically appeared next to him in the cell" he shook his head chuckling angrily
"it's not like that, " I said moving to stand in front of him, he narrowed his dark grey eyes at me and looked at my shirt (his shirt) and something flashed in his eyes but he didn't voice it. "Oliver called me after his arrest and that's when I left to the police station to bail him out" I was practically

begging him to believe me
"She is right, I called her to bail me out. that's all," Oliver said walking inside and stood next to the dining table.
"why her?" he asked pissed at him "why didn't you call me? did you even consider the time when you call her and at the police station at that" he yelled making us flinch
"I didn't know you were back in town," he said shifting nervously in his feet, "but you're right, I shouldn't have involved her" he sounded apological but Dimitri narrowed his eyes and looked between both of us and huffed "you are 27 years old Oliver act your age for one fucking minute" he cursed tightening his grip on his beer bottle. he was breathing hard in anger.
"I don't know what is going on between the two of you, but at least don't get caught" with that he left us standing in the kitchen in confusion and frustration, I gripped my hair in frustration and marched up to him and roughly pulled his arm stopping him on his way.
"Nothing is going on between us," I said clenching my jaw "I went because he needed my help," I tighten my grip on his arm and he glanced at his arm and raised an eyebrow, I let go of his arm and stood straight
"I don't care what you do behind my back or who you do Erika," he said with such ease, it hurts, it so fucking hurts.
" I'm gay," Oliver yelled after watching how intense our fight had gotten
Dimitri looked at him stunned and then back at me, I tried not to look too smug.
"I'm gay," Oliver said again but normally this time "I got into a fight with some homophobic scum and ended up in the cell, I didn't know whom to call and since Erika knew about me, made it easier to choose," he explained in one

breath looking at Dimitri expectantly.
his expression changed. from angry to hurt and then betrayed, he usually doesn't show any kind of emotions but here, right now. he was overflowing with it. "when?" he asked looking at his brother
"what?" Oliver asked him confused
"When did you know?" he asked gripping his beer bottle tightly in his hand, I was afraid it might break into pieces with the force he was applying, I moved aside so they can talk properly, Oliver had kept his secret for years and now was the first time he was accepting his sexuality in front of his family member
"When I was 12 years old" he mumbled not making any eye contact with his brother.
"When did you know?" this time the question was shot towards me, I shifted in my feet " after we got married," I said, he let out a harsh breath and walked away.
"well, that didn't go too well" Oliver commented sitting on the couch in the living room
"there's a first ade kit in the guest room," I said smiled, and went to my bedroom, Dimitri was leaning to the railing of the small balcony of our room which was rarely used, he sipped his beer staring far away into the night, his body was tense and he looked troubled.
"He didn't mean for me to find out," I said standing next to him, he didn't even glance at me "I walked in on him in his clinic, before the rehearsal dinner " I explained and he just listened " he didn't mean to keep this from you, he just didn't know how to tell you" I reasoned with him on behalf of Oliver. "He didn't know how you would react, he was so scared when I walked in on him, he almost cried and begged me not to tell you, he wanted to be the one to tell you" he

just listened, never interrupting
"We were supposed to be best friends, we shared everything" his voice was low full of betrayal " is it because we are not related by blood? does he not think of me as his brother?" he asked, he was in so much pain. I have never seen him this vulnerable, I was holding myself back from hugging him, and god! I wanted to hug him so bad.
"You may not share the same parents but he is still your brother and he loves you like one," I whispered not wanting to cross the thin line between us which will always be there.
"If he did, then he wouldn't have kept such a big secret from me," he said looking at the dark sky which was slowing fading into a beautiful morning.
I glared at him at his words "Now, you are just being a hypocrite Dimitri" he looked at me stunned not expecting a reaction from me. "You too are keeping a huge secret from him, not just him but your entire family," I said moving my hand back and forth between us "This is a lie, our marriage is a lie" he kept looking at me but with a blank expression
"This has nothing to do with them," he said gulping down the last of his beer, I snickered amused and pissed
"So is his sexuality," he glared at me to just drop it but I continued, not knowing when I'll get another chance to vent out my frustration "This marriage is a lie, our relation is a lie, it's just a stupid contract"
We got married right after Vanessa and it was just a quick, family-only type of ceremony. To say our families were not happy would be a lie they were furious especially my mom because she had planned a huge party and everything along with Vanessa's wedding maybe she thought she had a lot of time but unfortunately that wasn't the case, they agreed later on because we were very persistent and didn't want

something grand.
I mean why do the grand thing when this wasn't even real. His grandparents, Mr. and Mrs. Price were happiest among the bunch. And so was my mother, she was quite surprised by me deciding to get married because she had always thought that I'd end up old and wrinkled and still be working with loads of computers, and maybe settle down some with the library guy that my mother thinks would be good for me because he gave out books for free.
I smile at that thought and looked at my wedding ring sitting on my ring finger, who knew I would look at it and feel so much love and so much pain at the same time, but you know what they say about Love. there is no Love without pain, whoever said that must have been arranged married as well or just not happy.
I sigh and get out of bed and looked at the room across from mine, the door was open so maybe be he was back. there was a noise of pots and pans turning from the kitchen so naturally, I followed, and there he was. a total adonis wearing a plain black apron and making an omelet for breakfast. I just stood there looking at the unreal scene in front of me, maybe be I was gawking because he felt eyes on him
he looked up at me and smiled, not like the one where your heart accelerates but the one where it looked forced. "Want some eggs?" he asked like it was the most natural thing to ask, after last night's drama I thought he would up and leave like always
"um- yeah, sure," I said and moved to get some coffee, I kept looking at him confused since he has never been like this before because every time we had a major fight he would leave and would need a strong reason to come back

and yet, here he is.
"Why are you still here?" I finally asked after much endurance, he sighed and placed the pan on the counter, trying to act not too rude but it's me so who am I kidding.
"This is my house too, you know," he said leaning on the counter to look at me, the tight shirt he is wearing is clinching his body like a second drink distracting me from my original argument
"Yeah, but you don't usually stay the night or the morning after," I said taking a sip from the coffee cup, the bitter taste was awakening. he didn't say anything so I continued "where is Oliver?" I asked and his jaw twitched
"Did you kick him out?" I asked but he didn't reply "is this still about last night, if it is then we already apologized," I said and he scoffed
"I bailed you out of jail, both of you in the middle of the night. you think it's something simple" he narrowed his grey eyes at me while clenching his hand.
"We already explained why we were there," I said in a low voice trying not to ignite a fire I can't put out.
"I don't care what happened between the two of you or what both of you were doing, but once it's out of the house it's my reputation that's on the line, not yours," he said anger dripping from his words and every word out of his mouth was piercing through my heart like a dagger.
"It's always the reputation for you isn't it?" I whispered hurt and he heard it I think I saw him flinch a little but if he did feel bad then he is a damn good actor because the poker look on his face didn't change.
"Yes, because that's the only thing that matters," he said emotionlessly, his words hurt me deeper than I thought.
"Do you even care about me?" I asked and that made him

look at me with a strange expression on his face. "Don't I matter?"
"No," he said his voice monotone, God! Do me a favor and drive that knife through my heart.
I sighed and placed my cup on the counter and left the kitchen but came back with an envelope in my hand, I threw the envelope in front of him and he stared at it for a second and then looked at me "I can't do this anymore"
"What's this?" he asked and picked up the envelope and opened it, but then threw it back with double the force. "What's the meaning of this?" he asked furiously his hands clenching and unclenching furiously, his jaw ticked and the fury in his eyes said another, story. For the money, I thought he cared about me but who am I kidding, when it comes to him all my assumptions go down the drain
"I can't do it anymore and I've already signed it" I opened the packet and took out a check with 4 million$ in it. "This is everything I owe you up till now"
I have never seen him so angry before, he was literary fuming "why now?" he asked lowly starting at the document like he was trying to set it on fire "there are only a few months left for the contract to end, so why now?
"I don't want to live a lie," I said with so much sadness that it could break anyone's heart "I don't think I can live as fake Mrs. Price, anymore"
he didn't speak for a whole minute and then said
"Very well, then"
The moment the words left his mouth I froze, I was ready for this, I was. but to hear it directly from his mouth was more painful and brutal than my guess. I didn't say a peep, nor did I argue, I waited for him to finish this torture for once and for all.

"But not today," he said and I let out the breath I didn't know I was holding "Today is papa and mamma's wedding anniversary and they are throwing a charity event as always, be their daughter-in-law for the last time, and then we are done" with that he threw the apron on the floor and stormed out of the kitchen.

he slammed the door out his way and the tires of his car screeched as he drove off, that's... that's when I lost my footing and fell on the marble floor. I didn't scream, I didn't cry, I broke down.

Do you remember you're first heartbreak? people say that first love always hurts, they leave a deep scar out their way and ruin it for whoever will be next. yeah, That. but just multiply it with 100 and that is the feeling I'm feeling right now, total vulnerability

I know that I got what I wanted but why the hell was I not relieved or happy? why do I feel empty? knowing he was never there, to begin with.

Silent tears fell out of my eyes, I didn't cry. no, my heart did.

Later that day I found Oliver in my office, I sighed 'this is the last thing I need right now. I opened my office door and strolled in and sat on my chair.

"When did you leave?" I asked him and he smiled sheepishly

"I left last night, I didn't know if he wanted me there," he said with a sad smile and I know the feeling.

"You could have informed me, I was worried," I said and opened my laptop, looking at what I was supposed to do today.

"Sorry," he said "never mind that, what about the event tonight? you still on?" he said to me like a child waiting to go to the carnival. can't believe this guy is older than me by

4 years.
"Yeah," I said and gave him a fake smile/ happy smile.
"Great," he said but kept moving his eyes "good because I invited Pete, " I looked at him unable to respond, Pete is Oliver's long-term boyfriend and if he is inviting him then it only means one thing.
"You sure about it?" I asked him "Pete doesn't like being your secret"
"I'm... I'm no longer keeping him a secret" he took in a deep breath "I'm ready to come out" and exhaled. I smiled at him genuinely this time.
"That's great, I'm happy for you," I smiled and held his hand in mine "And if things went south I will always be there for you, you hear me?" he smiled relaxed, and stood up to hug me
"I know, thank you for always being so understanding" I hugged him back tighter and this time I was the one who needed that hug the most, trying to glue my broken pieces together.
"I'll see you tonight," he said and with that, he left and I was alone all over again, sighing I went back to my work there was still some time left before the event.
When the clock struck 6 pm, it was time to go and get ready for the big day. I wore a simple but elegant burgundy off-shoulder gown and put on some light makeup and diamond stud earrings, I pulled my hair in an elegant bun.

Dimitri was already there so, I had to drive my car, sighing I locked the door and was about to get in my car when out of nowhere a honk of a car. I jumped not expecting that and found a black Mercedes parked out our lawn, it honked again but the door of the driver's side opened and walked out a man in a black suit, at that moment there was only one thought in my mind.

Black Magic exists because I am completely bewitched.

"Let's go, you are late," Dimitri said monotone, I know I shouldn't look for compliments but at least you look nice wouldn't kill him, nodding I get in and we drove off.

the tension in the was thicker than smoke and choking, but I endured it. this was probably the last time we will be in the same car, as we parked inside the old mansion's parking lot, he didn't get out immediately, so I took it upon myself and opened the door.

"Don't tell anyone about what happened today we will end it quietly," he said calmly, I didn't reply just walked away.

The Price Mansion was buzzing with joy and happiness, it was torcher. they were too happy it was annoying but I held it in and faked a smile to everyone who greeted me and posed for media who were shooting the grand charity event. Dimitri was behind me but when the photographer asked for our couple picture I hesitated, my smile probably flattered a little but he was a pro, in the game of lies he was a king. he pulled me to him by my waist like it was the most natural thing he did, I gasped lightly. everywhere he touched my skin tingled, he held my waist possessively, like showing ownership in some weird way I liked it. I liked the attention he was giving me even if it was a little while.

"There are my babies" Mrs. Price exclaimed happily, the moment between us was gone and he let me go, Mr.Price was not far behind.

Adeline or Mrs. Price is in her late seventies, and Robert her husband was also the same. they are Dimitri's grandparents. he was raised by them from the age of fifteen, his parents died in a car crash and he was the lone survivor. Oliver is

his first cousin from his father's side Dimitry is the eldest child.
"You look, lovely darling," she said hugging me and Dimitry
"You look stunning Mamma as usual" I complimented her because it was true for someone who is in their early seventies she was so maintained "You look, handsome Papa," I said and he hugged me too and kissed my forehead
"You look beautiful my chid," he said smiling
"Happy anniversary guys, "Dimitri said with a small smile, he was not very close with his grandparents but he loved them but couldn't express his feelings
"I don't want your wishes" Adeline huffed dramatically "We are getting old and before it's too late I want to at least once hold my great-grandchildren"
Can you hear the sound of someone choking? yeah, that's me. Never in a million years have I ever thought of choking on absolutely nothing.
"Oh, my dear. are you alright?" Adeline rubbed my arm in means to calm me down. ha, like that's gonna work
All I could do was nod, "Adeline, stop scaring the poor child" Rober said amused with my reaction.
"All I said was that I want a great-grandchild, it's been more than 4 years, Rober," she said it might not be her intention but that kind of hurt, I cannot give them that happiness. I'm not Jane the virgin for christ's sake. I can't give a great-grandchild without doing IT
"Mamma, the event organizer is waving at you to go over," Dimitri said and pulled away from me and I could finally breathe.
I excused myself and went away in search of the bar, I need some serious liquid courage to get through this night.

"Hello, What can I get you to miss?" the young bartender asked politely smiling, I took a seat on one of the bar stools "Marchesi di Barolo Arneis 2013, please, "I ordered
"Coming right up" he smiled again and I waited for my drink, "Here you go, enjoy" I twirled around in my stool and watched everyone. some were old faces, some were new but many were reporters. unintentionally I was seeking someone out and you already know who. I found him talking to a group of people who screamed money with a capital M but what irritated me was the way one of the women was holding his arm and occasionally rubbing it, I felt a little twitch in my eye but suddenly my view was blocked.
"That's my seat," said a male voice, I raised my head to look at the vision blocker and raised an eyebrow in annoyance.
"Don't see your name on it?" I said sipping my wine he chuckled and sat on another stool beside me.
"Boy, the event hasn't even started yet and you are already in a bad mood" I didn't even glance at him. not worth it but he is kind of cute with blonde hair, blue eyes, tanned skin, and a red Armani suit. "I'm usually the one sitting gloomily in this corner, Name's Peter by the way," he said and I nodded at him, not in the mood to engage in a conversation "you don't want to be here, don't you" he chuckled again at my ignorance.
"Nope!" I replied popping up the p and finished my glass, "Refill," I said and passed my glass and took another, I glanced back at Dimitri again and almost broke the glass in my hand with the force I held it. Dimitri was now dancing with the woman who was seducing him just moments ago, people have no shame, I mean he is a married man leave him alone.
"Ah," Peter exclaimed like something finally clicked and

chuckled "You have hots for the ladies man, now I get it," he said sipping his drink
"It's not that," I said chugged down my drink and asked for another
"of course, of course" he laughed "You just "like him, " " he raised both of his hands to show the double-quotes.
"He is my husband," I said and he chocked on his drink
"What!?" he asked bewildered "You are Dimitri's wife? you are Erika Price?" he asked and I looked at him confused, "Dimitri and I, we are sorts of friends and small business partners " he explained and I nodded glancing back at Dimitri again but only to find him a lot closer to that woman than before. Peter watched my expression and said "You should go there and prove him yours" I stood up from my seat and grabbed the bottle of my wine
"It's not worth it" that I walked off. I took a huge gulp from the bottle and walked outside to the backyard, which did not go unnoticed by Dimitri. he watched my every move, I stared at him and we were caught in a staring match. I made sure to show mine displease while doing so it doesn't matter anyway it all ends today.
I walked across the backyard towards the pool and sat down, threw off my high heels, and submerged my feet in the icy cold water, drinking straight from the bottle. "I'm seriously so fucked up" I sighed and laid down on the floor with my legs still in the water, time passed by and the bottle dried up, not a single drop was left. I felt the buzz of alcohol in my system and felt it taking its toll on me, my vision was blurry and I felt so light. the sound of footsteps approaching my way alerted me and I looked to my left, big black boots stood a couple of feet away from me.
It's a man, he who-ever-he-is sighed in irritation and

crouched down, he held my arm to pull me up but I slapped it way "Hey, back off. I'm married," I said standing up wobbly, he didn't say anything just stood there, I couldn't see his face clearly because of my blurry vision but he seemed to be a good-looking guy. I swayed a little in my efforts to get away from the unknown man.

he caught my arm and steadied me, I pulled my arm out of his grasp but he held on tighter and pulled me closer to him, and bend down to pick me up bridal style. "Hey, stop it. put me down before I scream " I warned him, he ignored me and started walking away " You don't know who I am, I will scream and the bodyguards will break every bone in your body and-"

"Erika," he cut off my ramble and that voice was familiar, his chest vibrated when he spoke and the way my heart sped up confirmed my doubt

"Dimitri,"

"Dimitri," I said raising my head to look at his face, I could make out his facial features due to all the lights. his face was stone cold and he stared straight ahead, I stared at his face, unknowingly my fingers were hovering over his perfect jaw, but even with all that alcohol in me couldn't bring myself to touch his face, he is like this forbidden fruit that I can't have even if I wanted too.

With that thought, I sighed and dropped my hand, Dimitri glanced down at me but didn't comment and continued to walk ahead with me still in his arms.

"Why are you here?" I asked him breaking the awkward silence. "Shouldn't you be in there dancing around your bimbo?" my words were mixed but the jealousy in my voice was as clear as the day or... night.

He sighed "I was just trying to be polite" I didn't expect him

to explain but it was nice that he did
"Polite and flirty are two different things" I mumbled closing my eyes as a bright light flashed on my face
"Why are you drunk? you don't like to drink" he asked shifting me in his arms as he tried to open the passenger-side door of his car
"I'm scared" I whispered when he lowered me on the seat and put on my seatbelt, he paused and looked at me, his face was close and his scent was so alluring, it was getting hard for me not to lean forward and just kiss him to fulfill my desire before its too late.
"Of what?" he asked me his breath smelts like peppermint and whiskey, a very seductive combination
I didn't reply, I couldn't. so, I did what I have been wanting to do for a very long time. I leaned forward and kissed him, he froze but I moved my lips against him, tasting that divine flavor of sin on his lips.
I placed my right hand on his cheek moving impossibly closer, he didn't respond, not that I expected anything different but it hurt more than expected, maybe I need to stop this torture on myself. I pulled away and chuckled sadly
"Let's go home, I'm tired," I said pushing him out and closed the door.
he didn't move for a while but got in the driver's side after a minute or two, we drove back home in a crispy silence, I kept looking out the window and tried hard to keep my tears at bay.
"I don't hate you," he said glancing at me while driving, I saw his reflection on the window but didn't look at him.
I chuckled angrily "Yeah, you just don't love me," I said roughly wiping my fallen tears, he faced looking at me but I didn't turn

"And you do?" there was an edge in his voice that made me look at him, he was intensely staring at me waiting for my answer, I was about to reply when I looked behind at the window on his side and my eyes widened

"Watch out" but I was too late, but the truck had already smashed into our car and sent us flying away. the car rolled upside down and the glass of my window shattered on my face, I couldn't keep my eyes open, I struggled to look at Dimitri and I screamed looking at his face, blood seeped from his head and he was unconscious, his only support was the seatbelt but it was digging in his stomach, I pulled at my seatbelt but it was stuck, I tried harder and it came off, I crawled out from the shattered window and with lot difficulty, I crawled my way towards his side.

with tears running down my face I slowly undid his seatbelt and he fell almost hitting his head on the steering wheel, I pulled both of his arms trying to get him out of the car but something hit the back of my head with a lot of force, painfully before I lost my consciousness I turned to face my attacker and cursed

Peter held a gun in his right hand and smiled creepily before he pointed the gun on my face and pulled the trigger.

"And you do?" Dimitri asked me in a challenging manner, looking on the road ahead and not spearing me a glance. I chuckled in a very good mood

"Of co--" I tried to reply but the words seemed to stick in my mouth, I kept trying to say those words but nothing came out.

"Why don't you answer me?" he asked angrily clenching his jaw and not just talking but it was getting difficult for me to breathe as well, I held my throat trying to talk but the pressure was too much. "why?" he turned his head in my

direction and I screamed wordlessly
Blood seeped out of his head and down his beautiful face, his face was turning pale, his cheeks hollow, then his eyes turned lifeless. "Do you love me, now?" he asked in a very hollow and scary voice that did not belong to him. slowly his face was decaying right in front of my eyes and there was nothing I could do, I tried to move forward to touch him, feel him, hug him, but my body was glued in its place
"Yes" I chocked on my words but it came out bearly as a whisper and everything was getting fuzzy, slowing my vision was fading away from my husband
The last thing I heard before I lost consciousness was "Too late"
I kept struggling to breathe, gasping, choking, and all sorts of things but no use
"We are losing her," said a voice from a distance, I could not feel my body, I was floating in the abyss, I had no control over anything and for some strange reason I didn't want to too, I wanted to give everything up and just let go.
"she is going into cardiac arrest," the same voice said again, suddenly I felt a shot of electricity through my body and then again, and again.
I shot up from where I was lying and inhaled a huge amount of air, lights blurred my vision, there were ao many people and so many machines, I started panicking, my body shook in fear.
"Hey, hey, stay with me alright," a familiar face came into my vision and he held my hand "It's gonna be ok, you are ok," then slowly everything faded but before I was swept into the darkness I said one word
"Dimitri,"
Pain, the pain in my head and different parts of my body

woke me up, a slow beeping echoed in the room, groaning I hesitantly opened my eyes, everything was painfully white, I laid on a hospital bed, wearing a hospital gown, plaster on my right leg and left arm, an IV attached to my left hand along with heart monitor, what shocked me was the two people in my room. Mom and Vannessa were leaning on the couch at the end of the small room.

As I attempted to move the heart monitor spiked up, alerting my family. mom looked up and ran to me, she burst into tears and hugged my non-plastered body. Vannessa sat next to me opposite to mom and cried holding my arm.

"Thank god, baby, you are alright" mom cried looking at me holding my face in her wrinkled hand "I was so scared, I thought I lost you too" she wept but I couldn't remember why? then like a flood. everything came to me, the party, dancing, pool, being in his arms, the car, the question, and the crash.

My eyes widened in shock and fear, I gasped from all the pain and pressure the memories brought me. I looked at my family alarmed.

"Dimitri, Where is he?" I asked both of them but they cried harder, panic slowly flew in my body and I looked at them scared "Where is he?" I asked again but no reply, having enough of it I pushed my body to get out of the bed and ripped the IV out, blood dripped from my hand as every bone in my body screamed in protest but I didn't stop.

"Baby, please lie down. you will rip open your stitches," My mom begged but I couldn't stop. my plastered leg gave out and I fell, painfully. the door to my room opened and Oliver walked in

"Erika!" Oliver yelled before he came to my ade and helped me up, "What are you doing? go back to bed" he said I

looked at him, he was wearing his doctor's coat, but his face looked tired and his eyes were swollen red.
" Dimitri, take me to him, I need to see him now," I begged him, his face turned pale and sadness took over him. he didn't reply just kept glancing at my mother and sister who cried silently. "Answer me, god, damn it" I yelled holding his collar, a lone tear fell from his eye and he started shaking "He... he-" he stammered while replying, I tightened my hold on him "He is gone" when the words left his mouth I staggered back losing my footing, "Erika," he pulled me before I fell again
"No, no, no" I mumbled shaking my head denying what I heard
"I'm sorry," he cried holding my hand tighter, "I'm so sorry" he cried harder
"You're lying, " I whispered "you are lying" I screamed when he kept apologizing over and over again and slapped him
He didn't say anything just stood there, I inhaled deeply "How?" I asked trying hard not to breakdown
"Your car exploded after the crash, you were outside but he... he burned with it" Oliver choked while trying to control himself
A shiver ran down my spine when the vision of the car crash swept into my head, I closed my eyes but Dimitri' face covered with blood was the only thing on my mind
"Take me to him," I demanded to stare at Oliver. he shook his head "Please, I need to see him" I begged my voice was barely above a whisper. he looked pained but nodded and went out of the room.
My mom wiped my cheek and I then realized that I had been crying "It's ok my child, cry" she whispered hugging me

close to her body "Mamma's got you" and then I did.
I cried
Pain, regret, guilt, and many more emotions were overwhelming within me as I stood before a huge box where laid Dimitri or his completely crisp burnt body. my hands shook as I placed them on top of the box, tears fell down my cheek continuously and I wept in helplessness.
"I'm so sorry," I whispered in a thick voice, doctors made me wear a mask and a special suit because the cause of death was the fire. I leaned my head on the box and cried " I'm so very sorry, Dimitri, I wish it was me and not you" I wept for a long time before I was forced outside the morgue by Oliver.
"Did you find it?" I asked desperately with a tear stain on my face, Oliver looked stressed and avoided the eye contact. "The guy I told you about, Peter something. he was at the party and the accident site" he sighed and rubbed his face exhausted
"I've gone through every footage of the party and there is no one like you described, Erika" he explained painfully, I knew he didn't believe me because they think and the symptoms show that I'm going through PTSD but that's not the whole story.
"Oliver you need to believe me, I saw him, he was there that night, he hit my head with a gun" I almost yelled out "I know what I saw," I said leaning on my wheelchair, tears of desperation escaped my eyes and I'm too tired to control it "I know" I whispered closing my eyes.
Oliver kneeled and held my hands in his "I believe you, Erika, I do but we don't have enough or any proof that the guy was at the party or was at the site" he tried convincing me, I nodded in understanding

"I know," I said trying to make my words seem convincing
"Good," he said standing up and looked at his watch "I have got to go, but I'll be back in an hour, and besides your mom and Vennassa will be here soon," he said and wheeled me to my room, he carefully picked me up and laid me down then connected the IV drip. "I'll be back, " he kissed my forehead and looked at me sympathetically "Do you want something?" he asked me and I smiled
"I need my phone and my Laptop with wifi connection," I said, he nodded and left
Just because he didn't find anything does not mean it's not there, I'm gonna find him and when I do, he's gonna pay.
It's been hours and I'm still going through every bit of the footage and still not able to find anything, but I know it's there somewhere I just got to look for it. I've also contacted one of my friends from college and he agreed to help, he hacked into the security cameras from all around the accident site, and I have hacked into every news, social media, and paparazzi's pages to try to just get a little glimpse of Peter, I'm not sure if it's his real name but whatever.
I tried looking for the bartender that served us that night as well but he's a ghost now, no signs of him ever being there. it all seems to be like a setup and nothing is in sync everything happens to be in a perfect alignment like someone from the inside is involved but who can it be?
"Did you find anything?" I asked Lucas, my friend, from college on the phone, as I kept scrolling on my computer
"Yeah, I've mailed it to you, you need to see this," he said and disconnected
I opened my main and clicked on the recent one from him, I frowned staring at the photo, it was of me and Dimitri at the party, my heart clenched painfully at his perfect smile

but I have to get a hold of myself, contrarily in the background stood Peter staring at us from behind and there stood Margret beside him, she wasn't looking at the front but I knew it is her because I never liked her. I swear if she has anything to do with Dimitri's- Dimitri's Death, I will personally rip her to shreds.

I picked my phone and called Lucas "We need to take care of this quietly, no one can know," I said

"Are you sure you want to do this?" he asked hesitantly

"I might temporarily be crippled and can't help much but I have to do this, I need to know the truth behind that night," I said staring at Peter's face with so much hate that is enough to burn him alive.

"We'll find it, Erika, I promise," he said and disconnected, the reason he is the only one helping me is that we were a nemesis during our college time, always fought for the first place but this was the first time I approached him first and he didn't waste any time, he ran to me when he heard my voice, my voice filled with grief and pain and the Erika, he knew never cried.

I gathered my best security guards and bodyguards who fortunately happened to be ex-military. I also threatened Oliver to give me an early discharge. After a lot of persuasions, he agreed, Lucas and I made a plan to interrogate Margret.

Josh, my head of security arranged for us to easily continue with our plan, Margret was brought to a warehouse on one of our properties, she was tied to a chair looking terrified. good

"Mrs. Price, why am I here? why are you doing this?" she asked me shivering with fear

I gave her a warning look "I'm not in a good mood, Margret

and now, I'm gonna ask you a few questions and if you lie, I will cut your pretty fingers off your hand," I said signaling one of my guards to show her a knife.
She screamed and cried "I'll tell you, I'll tell you everything but please don't hurt me" she wept.
Nodding I wheeled myself towards her "Good, do you know this man?" I asked showing Peter's photo on my phone.
"Yeah, That's Albert, we met at a bar and I invited him to be my plus one," she said still shivering "I promise that's all I know, I have never seen him before and don't know what he did" she stuttered
I shared a look with Lucas and raised an eyebrow, Albert? looks like he goes by many names "Why did you invite him if you didn't know him?" I asked
"He was nice and said he works with Mr.Price, he told me he was invited so I suggested we go together instead," she said breathing a little normally.
I nodded "ok, I believe you for now if I find out that you are hiding something from me, you better watch out," I warned her and she nodded her head repeatedly.
later it was just Lucas and me along with a couple of guards, "What should we do now?" Josh asked me and I pulled out my laptop.
"And now, we run facial recognition," I coded the necessary code and waited for a match
"ahem," Josh cleared his throat and I looked at him "It's time," he said monotone
I paused in my movement, all the anger, energy, and fury I had in me vanished. it was replaced with immense pain in a fraction of seconds "Is it?" I whisper asked and he nodded. he placed his hand on my shoulder "It's time to say

goodbye," then a tear slipped my eye
Shh...listen, don't you hear?
I'm crying, but they are silent tears.
I'm crying on the inside so you can't see
all the pain running through me.
I cry for you, I cry for me.
I cry for the times I can't,
so if you listen, you may hear my silent tears.

-Amanda smith

The sky weeps for me and so does the grass, the world filled with joy is weeping in tears. I wish I could not feel this... this sadness, this fear.

People in the black walk up to me with sad faces or white roses, some hug me, and some just smile sadly, all I could was lean on my wheelchair and hold my broken pieces together. it's hard, faking to be ok, is hard.

"Oh, my baby," Adeline wrapped her arms around and cried, she embraced in her warm body and wept for her grandson, her only grandson who was the last connection she had to her son. I can't relate to the pain she is feeling and here she was trying to console me, a brave soul she is. silent tears slip out of my tired eyes and I held her tighter because she needed it more than I do.

"Adaline, please don't stress her out, she is already a wreck," Robert told his wife and gently pulled her away from me, he kissed me on the head and patted my back, "Be strong my child, " with a sad smile he moved away to attend some more guests.

I wheeled myself closer to the cascade that was sitting on

top of the hole in the ground waiting to be let down, I placed my hand on top and laid my head on it "I didn't answer your question" I whispered into the wooden cascade "I never said I loved you because I do, I love you so, damn much. so much that it hurts, and I never got a chance to say it," I cried wetting a patch. "I promise to find out what happened that night, I promise to make them pay" I kissed the cascade and moved back

I watched the cascade being lowered into the ground as the priest kept on talking, I know what he is saying but couldn't seem to concentrate, I watch him being lowered into the ground where he will rest for good, tears flowing freely down my face and I couldn't seem care.

I was handed a handful of soil and was asked to pour on top of the lowered cascade, I do it and promise myself to avenge him.

"I Love you, Dimtri, I always have and always will." I throw a red rose as well before kissing it.

Everything happened so fast, and it was time for the service. I met some more people before excusing myself to go rest, John helped me up to Dimitri's room in the mansion. I thanked him and explored his room in my wheelchair.

It was not a typical teenager's room, the walls were dark grey, with a king-size bed, study table, couch, walk-in closet, and a huge window. this room is on the third floor so the view was breathtaking, I was so engrossed in the view that I didn't hear Robert come in.

"I was going to grill that window, you know?" he said in a warm, heavy voice he walked to stand beside me looking through the window as well

"Why?" I asked because he paused

He smiled sadly like he was recalling a memory "Dimitri was

a stubborn teen, always snuck out in the middle of the night even though his room was this high above" he chuckled "no matter how many guards I assign to stop him but it was all in the vain, he would somehow always trick them, so one day I followed him, " I looked at him raising an eyebrow "I know what you are thinking, I thought he was getting involved with the bad crowd but I was proven wrong" he smiled tearing

"where did he go?" I asked playing with my fingers

"He went out every day in the middle of the night to see his parents," he said and stopped talking

And I knew, why?

Dimitri went to the graveyard to his parent's grave, and now he laid beside them.

"He knows you love him," I said he smiled down at me

"And he knows you love him, "that he left while patting on my shoulder on his way out.

I sat there silently for maybe an hour and then moved towards the bed, the room was cleaned so I can rest here and I was grateful but sad because now I don't smell him here, to distract myself from going there again. there were a lot of pictures on a wall.

Dimitri with his grandparents, friends, and Oliver but all of them were from his teenage years and up, but not a single picture of his younger self. I pulled out a smiling picture of him he might be 20 or something, I pulled it closer to myself and drifted off to sleep.

The next day came painfully slow because I kept waking up in the night with cold sweat, racing heart, and burning lungs. somehow the night was over and the sun came shining through the wide window, onto my face. it was a beautiful morning but there was a heavy sorrow in the atmosphere.

shaking away those bad thoughts, I pulled myself in the wheelchair and went to the bathroom to do my morning business.

After being freshly showered I tried walking holding the wall for support, limping I stood in front of his wardrobe, opening it I was enveloped in his divine fragrance. his smell still lingered on his clothes, they were old maybe from his teenage years before he left for college but they will fit, he has always been huge and fit.

After changing into one of his shirts and short pants, with the help of John, I wheeled down for breakfast in the dining room. Adaline, Robert, Oliver, Pete, and Oliver's parents, and some more family members having a silent breakfast stopped and stared as I made my way to an empty chair next to Adaline.

"Good morning, darling, how did you sleep?" she asked kissing my forehead, her stare lingered on my clothes and her eyes moist with dull recognization, she smiled and I returned it.

"I slept well, how about you?" I asked and smiled at a servant who served me breakfast.

"Good," she went back to her plate and gracefully chewed on her slice of bread.

I glanced at Oliver, he was helping Pete by pouring coffee into his cup, the love around them was painfully good and refreshing, I turned my head to look at his parents to see their reaction to his behavior, they were tense but it was not something to poke into anyways.

Breakfast was uneventful and awkward, well that much was expected.

My phone rang bringing me out of my train of thoughts

"Lucas?" I asked waiting for him to speak.

"I found something"
The moment Lucas utter those words I wheeled myself to Dimitri's room and opened my laptop to check what he has found. there was a new link in my mailbox and on opening it there was a criminal report about a person name X next page consisted of a photograph of the person with many names, Peter or Alber, or someone along the lines.
The photograph was a candid one where he was smoking a cigarette leaning on a car, it was a bit blurry maybe taken from far away, anyways there are many cases filed against Mr.Unknown and all of them were somehow closed and none of them were solved. there was extortion, murder, kidnapping, and drug trafficking looks like Dimitri got caught in something he shouldn't have
I called Lucas "What happened to facial testing? did you find any location?" I asked him as I logged into the national security database, It's not easy but It's not that difficult as well.
He sighed "It takes around more than 3 months for the location to pop up, Erika, you know that," he sounds tired and that made guilt shot up within me, I'm so engrossed in finding the truth that I didn't consider his wellbeing, I'm such a terrible friend.
"I'm sorry, Lucas, I didn't mean to be so impatient with you, I just want to know what happened that night," I said feeling sad and disappointed
"I know, Erika, I know," he said with pity clear in his voice, I didn't want anybody's pity I just want the truth and as soon as possible.
After a short depressing talk with him, we hung up. Facial recognition may indeed take more than 3 months due to a large population throughout the world so I had to wait, no

matter how much it kills me I had to wait
so, that's what I did
For six months.
Six months, it took six months for us to find X's exact location, that bastard was hiding in Brazil, Rio.
I was completely healed in those six months, physically at least. My family was worried about my behavior after the accident, they thought it was PTSD and even got me to go to therapy. I know they are worried about my wellbeing but I needed space, they keep hovering above me and always checking up on me which is nice and all but they need to understand that I need closure.
I know I have turned it into a very unhealthy obsession, and it will stop, eventually. that is after I find that son of a bitch and beat the truth out of him.
Everything we found about him in these six months is that he is a very powerful man, and powerful men are often dangerous, he is one of the most dangerous mafias in the world and would stop at nothing to gain what he is after.
With that said I packed my bags and took off to Brazil to find the person responsible for my husband's murder.
I arrived at The Rio international airport at midnight, John and Lucas were with me. I want to bring them with me because I know the risk but yet, they would not leave me alone. they care about me more than I knew
"I've already booked a hotel nearby, we'll rest for now and look for him in the morning," Lucas said hiking up his duffle bag and I nodded
We got changed and had dinner after we reached our hotel, all of us were jetlagged but none of us were sleeping. we were submerged with the thoughts of tomorrow, we had a plan but none of us were prepared, we had no experience in

this area.
all kinds of what if's? surrounded me but exhaustion won and I drifted off to another dreamless night.

"He is usually here on Tuesdays, to check on the business, I guess," Lucas said nodding towards a shabby-looking apartment building in front of us, we have been observing this building for half an hour.
waiting for Mr.Unknown.
The first thing we did when we found his location was to track his routine and fit it into our database, what he does? where he goes? where he lives? what does he eat? everything.
After observing him enough, we head out to take matters into our own hands. We didn't contact the police here because he controls the police here, which came as a shock to us since we didn't realize how dangerous this man can be.
"here he comes, " Lucas said staring at a black limo. Peter got out of the backseat and stood tall like some kind of a King.
It makes my skin crawl with just looking at him, for a murderer, he looks at so much ease, no regrets, and no remorse.
"let's go," I said and moved swiftly Lucas stood back for backup. John and I moved to the fire exit to go unseen.
"Remember, don't kill anyone we just need to observe and don't get caught," I ordered John and he nodded in understanding.
We climbed up to the topmost apartment of the building and watched from the window. Peter was in there surveying the weapons and drugs displayed on the tables. Lots of scary-looking men with lots of tattoos were guarding the

place.
I make eye contact with John we nod. we secretly take pictures of Peter and all the illegal things around the apartment. we wait for a while and before anyone sees us we got out of that place.
When we safely reach the bottom of the fire exit and Lucas was waiting for us in a black car. "What did you find?" he asked us as we got in the car.
"Something illegal," I said monotone and pulled out my laptop. I linked all the pictures and videos we captured and sent them to the higher, uncorrupted detectives.
"Now what?" Lucas asked
I sighed leaning onto my seat "Now, we wait"
The police are the police and took their time to reach the crime site, Peter had already left when they arrived but we were smart. we followed him silently in our car and drove off to somewhere into a remote area.
it was getting dark as we drove behind Peter's limo, we were smart not to turn on our headlights so they could figure out they were being followed. after 2 hours of driving the limo slowed down in a completely abanded place.
our location was being traced by my trustworthy detective back in America. so, we were safe, or at least if we die our bodies would be found.
The limo drove into a smaller road and entered a huge metal gate which opened automatically. I held Lucas's hand when he was driving towards the gate as well.
"Cameras," I said nodding towards the top of the wall where there was a camera. if there are sensors there will be cameras.
John and I got out "Stay hidden if we don't come out within 2 hours call backup or leave," he looked like he wanted to

argue but didn't and nodded.

I signaled John to follow me and we walked to a secure place where I could climb the wall and disable the cameras manually there were three cameras on the wall as well but were at quite a distance.

After successfully disabling the first two cameras we jumped off the wall and quietly ran in, there were guards at every corner but John being the muscle among us took care of that. we ran towards the voices and stood in front of a huge window.

Peter was talking to someone but it was not clear who, maybe a partner or someone of higher authority because it looked like he was explaining something. the other guy pulled out a gun and pointed at Peter who looked scared shitless. John and I shared a look of confusion but kept quiet.

Then that changed the position of his gun and shot Peter's guard Dead, in one shot.

I flinched at the sound, John placed his hand on my shoulder in comfort to which I was grateful, but then the guy with the gun pointed the nozzle at Peter and spoke like he was warning him.

and then he turned.

My heartbeat stopped, and I froze in my place so did John. the person stood in front of us was none other than

Dimitri

he didn't look a day older than the last time I saw him, he was burnt to a crisp but now he's not. what the hell is going on?

unknowingly I stepped back and something fell, maybe a pot it broke creating a huge sound. everybody's attention snapped towards the window where we were and they

rushed to get to us. we ran and tried to get away but they had guns and dogs.
"Stop them," someone yelled as we ran towards the gate but before I could reach the gate someone hit my head and I fell, but before I closed my eyes I saw feet approaching me it felt like a Deja Vu but this was not it was not someone unknown, this time it was someone I loved dearly and someone I thought was dead.

Slowly I open my eyes but shut them quickly due to sharp light. I groan as pain shot through the back of my head.
"Good, you're awake," said a smug voice
I open my eyes again, blinking my eyesight adjusted to the view. I narrowed my eyes at the culprit sitting in front of me on a recliner, smugness never leaving his face.
"Hello, beautiful," he said smirking showing off his perfect white teeth, Peter.
I try to move but notice that I'm tied to a wooden chair, I pull at my restraints but to no avail, I feel a slight cut on my wrists so, I stop pulling at them and turn to glare at my captor.
"Ooo... don't look at me like that, it does something to me and it's not such a good idea, I don't want to die young," he chuckled amused which made me glare at him harder
"That's funny of you to talk about death, you killed my husband in cold blood," I spit at him but it still doesn't the look on his face.
"Husband," he laughed clenching his stomach like it was the funniest thing he has ever heard. I wait for him to finish
"You are so cute, Erika," he sobered up.
"Where are my friends?" I asked
"Don't worry about them, they are where they should be,"

he said walking out of the room, he turned around before he closes the door "Try to stay calm when you see him," that he locked the door.
I move in my place trying to loosen the restraints but they dig deeper into my skin. I sigh tired off. I close my eyes to try to calm my racing heartbeat. I didn't want to think about it but my mind goes off to the events of last night.
those familiar grey eyes, dark hair, sharp jawline, and that complete beautifully handsome face. the face of my husband. the same husband who died six months ago.
I drift off after a while and woke up when the room was completely dark except for the moonlight shining from the huge window, where there is a shadow of a man. he is looking out the window in deep thoughts
"I've always found the Fullmoon beautiful, it intensifies the beauty of nature," the first thing he says is a random thing about the moon.
I don't reply, even if I did reply I wouldn't know, how?
After a deafening silence, I speak " You died,"
he hummed in response and turns around to face me, I hold in a gasp because he looks breathtaking. he intensely stares at me "and yet, here I am" he opens his arms wide
"how? Dimitri, I saw you die, I held a funeral for you," I yelled with anger, guilt, and sadness.
"you are right, Dimitri did die, and you also held a funeral for him," he walks up to me and leans in so close that our foreheads almost touch. "But I'm not Dimitri," he whispers deadly low in a husky voice.
"What do you mean," I ask with equal intensity, we have never had this kind of sensuousness in our entire four years of marriage.
"That's none of your business, You came here because you

wanted to know what happened that night and now you do, so when you are out of here never come back and if you do, your friends die a very painful death," he warns in a husky low tone. It brings shivers down my spine, I've never felt this kind of tension in me before it is almost exciting.
"I don't know why you're doing this, why fake your death?" I ask and the moment is gone, he steps away from me.
"Because it was time for Dimitri to die," that he leaves and doesn't even turn back. it hurts but moreover it is confusing the shit out of me. what the hell is happening?
A couple of hours later three men wearing full black walk in and untie me. "What are you doing? what's going on?" I ask but it falls to deaf ears.
they pull me out of the room and carry me outside, I was too panicked to admire the castle-like house. I pull my arm back and headbutt the guy, he yelps in pain. I pull my free hand punch the other guy in the guts and kick the other in the balls. two of them wither in pain but the other one comes at me again and I stand in position ready to kick his ass.
he tries to punch me in the face but I dough and kick him instead, and finish him up with an uppercut. the other two looks at me annoyed and jump me together but I dough all their attacks and beat the shit out of them. all the anger, frustration, and sadness I was feeling was overpowering me.
"Stop it," A loud commanding voice yells and a group of guards surrounds me with guns in their hands. I was too far gone to heed their warning and took a step closer to the guy on my right.
"What's going on?" Dimitri asked in a scary voice, there was pin-drop silence, no one spoke. He walks up from behind

me and stares "What are you doing?" he asks but this time the question is directed to me.
I glare at him instead "I gave you a chance to leave and you do this," he gestures to the three bruised men "This is your last chance, Erika If you don't leave now. you can never leave," he threatens me but I stood my ground "very well," he says and in a swift movement, everything is upside down. "What the hell? Dimitri put me down, "I hit his muscular back but the man is built like a wall, "put me down right now-" I yelp when there is a sharp sting on my right ass cheek. "Did... did you just spank me?" I asked in horror, his shoulder vibrates as he chuckles.
we don't talk after that, he walks for a while and climbs a large staircase on the second floor. the second floor itself is vast and glamorous, all the walls have different kinds of paintings, Portraits, and statues. what intrigued me was portraits of a family. there is a beautiful couple with two children, one is a boy and there is a baby in the woman's arms. Dimitri walks faster into the corridor and stood in front of a dark wooden door, he opens the door and walks in then threw me on a bed.
I bounce where I land and it is the most comfortable bed I have ever seen, he walks around the room looking for something, I follow his every movement "Why am I here, Dimitri?" I ask
He stops what he was doing and marches towards me, he holds my jaw tightly and leans dangerously close to my face "Call me Dimitri one more time and I'll put this mouth to better use," he growls in my face there is a glint in his eyes that says he might do it.
I know it is supposed to scare me but it does something different, it makes me feel something I've never felt.

I feel hot, and it's not anger.

I don't remember getting in the car, nor do I remember walking down at the airport as if I found myself sitting on the flight way back home in a daze.
My world seems to be crashing down on me with a single piece of paper, I always thought God was punishing me for something I had done when I lost Dimitri that night at the accident but the bigger punishment was to face the person I thought I had lost forever only to lose him differently, again.
Engrossed in my thoughts I didn't see the flight attendant trying to get my attention, "huh?" I ask trying to regain complete consciousness
"Ma'am, we have landed, " She said with a forced smile, I nod my head and get up carrying my handbag because that's the only luggage they found on me when they caught us.
"Thanks," I say before departing, I walk out of the airport after all the checking done and hail a cab, going straight to my house the one I shared with Dimitri/Massimo.
On unlocking the door, a wave of loneliness washes down to me but I have run out of tears. I sat down on the couch and just stay like that for a couple of hours, no movement, nothing. finally, after gathering up some courage, I go to my room and start packing. I know it might seem different from an outsider's point of view but I'm no longer a part of the Price family so, no reason for me to be here. as I reached a certain box behind the shoe compartment it spiked my curiosity. I pulled a large size wooden box and dragged it a bit on the marble floor.
When I opened the box tears blurred my vision, It's my wedding dress along with everything I wore on that day, I

pulled it out and the beautiful white floor-length dress was as same as the day I wore it five years ago.

With a heavy heart, I packed everything I owned and left the rest, I was conflicted with what to do with the wedding dress, and an idea popped in my head. I placed as many boxes as I could fit in my car apart from the wooden box which sat on my passenger seat and drove off to the last place I wanted to be.

The Price Mansion.

After completing all the security clearance at the gate, I drove towards the entrance to the Mansion. I sat in my car holding the wheel and contemplating whether to do what I was to do or not.

Sighing heavily I got out and stopped the Valet before he reached for my keys. "Thanks, but I'm not staying for long," I say and opened the passenger side door. He rushed to me when he saw the size of the wooden box and I smiled at him gratefully.

A maid opened the door and smiled at me welcomingly, I nodded at her "Who's at the door, Stella?" Mrs. Price asked loudly when I walked towards where she was sitting she almost ran to me and engulfed me in a warm hug, a hug I have been craving all along. unknown to me a few tears slipped away and soon it got too intense.

She consoled me and some of her tears shed as well, we sat down after an emotional moment and settled down.

"How was your trip, honey," she asked pouring me some tea, as they were not a part of my scheme so they did not know my little stunt.

"It was eye-opening, I guess," I said with hidden meaning which she didn't push.

"Good, good, I liked the idea of a little fresh air for you, "

she smiled sadly at me and continued sipping her calming tea.
The valet bought my wooden box inside the grand living room and placed it on the ground next to the coffee table. Mrs.Price looked at me confused
"What's this, darling?" she asked leaning towards the box curiously, guilt clawed me from within
"Something I have no use for, "I said opening the box which made her weep a little with sadness.
"Why are you giving this to me? Don't you want something to remember him? all I have is a few photographs of him at least you have this," she cried. I sat beside her and tried to console her but stopped when her previous sentence said something about photographs
"You have all of his photographs?" I asked and she stopped crying ending with hiccups.
"Of course, I have my grandson's son photographs, what kind of grandmother would I be if I didn't?" she questioned me back
"Can I see them, please?" I begged her, she was not reluctant but complied, by the time she brought the albums I had one of the maids move the box to Dimtri's room.
Mrs.Price came back with a couple of albums and sat next to me and showed me Dimitri's pictures but there was one problem
"You don't have any of Dimitri's Childhood photos?" I asked looking through the album to only find high school pictures up until college and some recent ones.
My question seemed to sadden her even more, I hate myself for doing this to someone as old as her " Robert was against Trever's choice of a woman in marriage and they had a huge fight, which resulted in their separation. Trever had his

father's stubbornness so he married the one he loved and moved to another country he used to call me sometimes but never visited. days turned to weeks and then years. it took a toll on both of us when we got the news of Dimitri's birth, we wanted to get them back here but Trever refused to listen to us. he had started his own business and wanted to stay there for good, he might have hated us too much because he never told us his address." she whimpered at her painful memory. I held her hand supporting her breakdown "Robert doesn't show but he was hurt the most, after accepting our mistake we started living it but the accident happened and Dimitri being underage the child service contacted us and we rushed to get to Dimitri the fastest way we could, even after trying our best to provide for him he still treated us as strangers, we never blamed him for his behavior it was our fault since the beginning which we had accepted, up until now he was still distant towards us but that didn't upset me because he was with us and that's what mattered," she was wise and kind for a woman her age. she is a person who had lost her entire family in an accident and still stood strong.

As I analyzed every word she said a thought crossed my mind "do you have any of his parent's pictures? I don't think I've ever seen it," I say not seeming like a greedy bitch in front of a weeping mother

"I must have them somewhere," She said walking to her room for more photographs.

This time came back holding a single photograph in her hand "This is the only photo I have of them together " she said holding out the photo.

I take it carefully and on glancing at the picture only one thought came into my mind.

'he was right, he is not Dimitri price'
because they were not the same people I saw at his mansion.

After my short and emotional moment with Mrs.Price, I left Price Mansion went back to stay with my mother in my old house. she didn't push much for an explanation just hugged me and told me to use my old room upstairs, that's when I realized how strong my mother is. she lost the love of her life at a young age with the responsibility of two little girls and now to watch your younger child going through the same pain must be terrible. the only difference in our situation is that she had lost the love of her life and mine didn't want me.
I sighed unboxing the last box and I have officially moved in. I had such an emotional time that I need an escape a real one this time. so, I called my childhood best friend Nicole. she is very different than my other friends she is not nerdy and boring she is the opposite of that.
I press the call option and wait for her to pick up " Erika Julia Price, how dare you leave without a single text or a call. do you realize how worried I was when Mrs.B told me? huh?" she screamed in my ear my lips pulled in a small smile, finally, someone how didn't treat me like a fragile glass doll who might break with a little push.
"Hey, Nicky," I greeted not as loud, she was silent for a second
"I pick you up at 5," she said but she could hang up as always I told her to pick me up from my old house she agreed and that's how I ended up at a salon
According to the breakup guru aka Nicole Martinez, makeup and makeover solve everything. it was a good idea since I haven't had a proper hair makeover for almost a year,

the stylist loved my long dark hair so he kept it long but gave it a nice look. later I had to go through trimming, threading, waxing, and a full-body spa in approximately 5 hours. while I was going through the reincarnation, Miss. Nicole was busy shopping since according to her the full makeover was never complete without a proper dress but she joined me soon enough.

When the clock hit 10 pm Nicole forced me into a beautiful black short dress which was sort of decent for a widow (according to others but divorced according to me) and she wore a red bodycon which enhanced her hourglass figure, she is Afro-American with dark chocolate complexion, height 5'5, curly hair, and black eyes. she was considered the most beautiful girl in my high school she is also the prom queen, being an heiress gave her a lot of leverage so she had a business degree handling her own company.

"Ready?" she asked crazily excited making me chuckle and nod," say it, so I can hear," she yelled on top of her lungs and also the radio which played some rocking party song.

I smiled "Yes," I yelled joining her level of enthusiasm

"Then... Let's get this party started!" she yelled and drove towards our destination, for a moment I was scared to ride with her due to her dangerous driving and said to myself to 'suck it up and enjoy'

The Sin That's what the club was called and being the goody-two-shoes that I was, have never been to a place like this. the bouncer let us in when he saw it was Nicole Martinez, and me. I don't think he let us in because of me, that's for sure.

I looked at her and she smiled at me mischievously "This belongs to one of my ex-boyfriends," I looked at her disbelievingly "What, it was a mutual breakup and we are friends now," she tried to reason making me shake my head. typical Nicole, no one could hate her even if she broke their heart they would still bow down to her every wish.

As I scanned the area something didn't add up. this was not our regular club people were wearing minimum clothes and lots of people wore collars, people were wearing leather pants and no shirt, women were holding whips and there were people like us who wore regular party clothes. I looked at Nicole speechless as we made eye contact

"This is... this is..." I couldn't even say the words

"Yes, we are at a BDSM club" she smirked walking towards the bar area.

I was too shocked to go on my own so I followed her like a lost puppy, she spoke with the bartender ordering our drinks and I tried my hardest not to look at the guy who was only wearing a collar and a very, very small thing. yeah, a thong. Nicole has outdone herself

"Here, wear this do not take this off unless you want to have some fun," she suggestively wiggles her eyebrows. I scowled at her and took the red wristband from her hand.

"Why?" I asked wearing the wristband

"Well, the are some rules that need to be followed here, as this is not a regular club some people might only like to visit and just experience without doing anything sexual. the owner came up with these protective bands, there are three types of bands blue is for staff that indicates if they have consent they can wiggle," she winked at me silly, I chuckled at her antics and thanked the bartender for the vodka shot.

"There is a Green band that says they are ready to mingle and then there is a red band like yours," she said tapping the band on my left hand "That indicates that you are not interested in participating just visiting," she said before

downing her shot
Shrugging the weirdness of this place I let loose because I was happy about the band on my hand, I was safe.
As the night dragged on with lots and lots of alcohol in our system we were on top of the world, as my vision got blurry I felt free, and finally, I was happy. we danced till our feet hurt and drank till our stomach couldn't take it.
I was sitting on a stool at the bar counter and Nicole was nowhere to be seen, I had didn't realize before but she wasn't wearing any wristband maybe she went to get some while I was getting wasted.
"Ma'am, can I get you a cab? your friend might not be back anytime soon," The bartender said looking over me from his place
I waved him off using my left hand showing that I'm not interested in his offer, "I'm Not Interested," I tell him and he laughed as I told him some joke
"I know, I'm not asking for a lay. I'm asking so you can go home and wait for the serious headache to hit you," he joked smiling
I stared at him with my blurry vision I could only figure out his tall stiletto, he was very tall. suddenly the world seems to spin and bile raised in my throat.
"shit," he said and jumped across the bar counter to get to me, "please don't puke here, " He said and dragged me to what I assume a bathroom.
he opened one of the stalls and pulled me towards the toilet if I wasn't puckish before I was defiantly now due to the horrible smell in here. I puked my guts out as he held back my hair and soothingly rubbed my back.
after puking my guts out we sat on the dirty bathroom floor and leaned back, my vision cleared a bit and I can make out

a few of his features. he has dark hair don't know if it's brown, sharp jawline and sparkly white teeth that's when I saw his wrist, he wore an identical wristband to mine.
"So, cab?" he asked smiling brightly, so bright that it hurt my eyes and I groaned in pain making him laugh.
he has a nice laugh

"Please, stop running," the bartender said sighing behind as I took off in the street, after the show in the bathroom he dragged me out from the dirty stall and helped me get outside but it was so nice that I wanted to walk so, that's what I did.
"I don't know your name," he almost cried out in frustration and that had me burst into giggles, I don't know why but he was very funny.
"It's Erika," I yelled running on the dark empty street
"Erika let us stop running now so, that I can get you home," his words fell to deaf ears. I kept running and running, and running it was so beautiful and nice.
suddenly the world seemed upside down, I was hoisted upon his shoulder like a sack of potatoes. "Let go of me, you asswipe. I'm married" I yelled hitting his back as strong as I could but alas it didn't look like it hurt at all.
He didn't say anything just kept walking towards somewhere, I didn't do anything further and just hand there like a lifeless stuffed doll. it became darker as we moved further looking around I figured we were in the parking area and he was walking towards the bike section, which was not such a good idea.
He pulled me from his shoulder and dumped me on the seat of his bike. I pouted looking at him because he was not gentle while throwing me on the seat of the bike. he smiled

at me "Ok, now, tell me where you live so I can drop you off and be back to my normal life," he teased which make me giggles like a teenager.
"I live in Hogwarts, Hogwarts is my home," I said the line I have always wanted to, "You muggles cannot see it, it a hidden world," I said whispering the last worlds shushing him in the end, he held his mouth holding in his laugher but failing miserably.
"Ok, Ms.Hogwarts what do we do now?" he asked dramatically rubbing his chin, I burst into giggles again
"I don't know, I missed my train," I shrug sadly
"I have no other solution to our little problem, " he said climbing on the bike and pulled me to sit properly holding his waist tightly, but my arms slipped repeatedly and he sighed. he took off his jacket and put it behind my back and tied it across his chest which had me clinging to my like a second skin.
"Stop taking advantage of me Mr. muggle, I'm married," I remind him like a snoozer on an alarm
his laughter vibrated into his entire body "I don't take advantage of drunk married women, Ms.Hogwarts," he chuckled
He kicked his engine on and we took off into the night, I don't know if I was too drunk but it felt like I was flying and the world seemed so beautiful. the wind blew in my hair and kissed my flushed cheeks, shivers went down my spine and I have never felt so alive. I hugged him tighter laying my head on my shoulder and snuggled in, maybe this was not such a bad idea. with a smile on my face, I closed my eyes not worrying about what might happen next just living the moment.
I felt a buzz in my head and the pain grew with time,

groaning in pain I open my eyes only to shut them due to harsh light. I moaned in pain again but opened my eyes again and held my head as if it may fall off my shoulder.
"Good morning, Ms.Hogwarts," a voice so loud it almost split my brain in half.
"Shush," I said with a finger on my lips "Oh, you want me to be quiet?" he asked loudly making me glare at him.
"Please, shut up," I groaned again but got off the bed which wasn't mine in a room that was not mine either. I look at him and he is the same guy from last night "The bartender, right?" I asked pointing at him and he nodded
"Yup, that me. but that not all I'm to you," he said seriously pausing me in my moment to look at him with confusion
"We... I don't know how to say this..." he laughed nervously
"What?" I asked nervously trying to remember the events of last night but the hangover stopped me
"Well to put it bluntly..." he paused again, I gave him a nervous/impatient look. "We had sex," he said seriously, there was pin-drop silence in the room, all sounds except our breathing
I walked towards him shocked, he looked at me with pity
"I'm sorry I didn't mean to it just happened and you look so stunning..." I hit in on the back of his head and he started laughing.
"Very funny, " I snorted unladylike. "Lie better next time," I taunted him but he laughed so hard that he ended up wheezing.
I saw the bathroom door open and walked in without asking for permission because I knew he wouldn't mind. the bathroom was small and reminded me of my college dorm tiny space but it was enough to do the deed. there was a normal size mirror near the sink, I looked horrible, which

he called stunning. I was not wearing my clothes but in a large shirt, probably his, and short shorts which were tied with a shoelace.

I know I should scream bloody murdered on waking up in a stranger's room wearing his clothes but he didn't look like those people he was nice and friendly but not dangerous and I would have known if we did anything last night, being virgin and all have some advantage, you would know.

After I was done using the bathroom I walked to a small kitchen where Mr.Bartender was fixing up breakfast, I sat on the kitchen stool watching him swing his butt on the beats on the music basting on the mini speakers.

"Nice moves," I teased loudly to which he jumped surprised he laughed nervously "Thanks," he said blushing red "I have pancakes," he said holding up a plate and the aroma was mouthwatering it made my stomach grumble rather loudly.

"Someone's hungry?" he teased getting back to his old self

It was my turn to blush "sorry," he smiled serving me breakfast with coffee to healing my hangover.

"By the way, I never got your name," I said after inhaling the delicious pancakes and washing them down with coffee he smiled and passed me Advil, I smiled gratefully.

"It's Adrian, but everyone calls me Viper," he said, my head snapped up to watch him confused

"Like the car cleaner, wiper?" I asked him astonished.

he chocked on his food laughing "No, not Wiper, Viper you know? Like the snake." he explained and it was my turn to burst out laughing, I laughed till I couldn't take it

"Your parents really, hated you huh?" I asked chuckling and he smiled embarrassedly

"My father was in the Forest department and He loved snakes," he shrugged still embarrassed we stared at each

other and laughed out together hilariously.
"Oh, by the way, word of advice," he said as we were dressed and leaving his apartment when I got a call from Nicole she is guilty of leaving me and wanted to treat us with lunch as a truce. I waited for him to finish his sentence. "Next time don't go to that bar again, it not a place for women like you," he said walking to the street, I had called for a cab since I can't ride on his bike when I'm sober, long dress and all.
I stopped next to him looking at him questionable "women like me?"
He shrugged "You know, Women like... you," he gestured all of me to which I gave him really look. "I mean, like you. Married," he said opening the door of the cab when it arrived.
I stood there stupefied then raised my right hand to smile sadly at the missing ring.

I didn't speak the entire way to the mall where Nicole has invited me for lunch, I watched the road from the window thinking deeply about what had happened to me within 6 and a half months. My life has changed so drastically that I had never even imagined these things.
Adrian sighed "Look, I'm sorry I shouldn't have brought that up," he didn't know what was wrong with me, and yet he still apologized.
Signing I looked at him and smiled sadly It's true I was married for almost five years," I said rubbing my ring finger missing the feel of the platinum band. he waited patiently for me to continue "But, I lost him in an accident six months ago," he looked at me apologetically "Don't give me that look I'm tired of it," I said waving off his sympathetic

expression.
"Tell me about yourself, I don't know anything about you, yet you know all about my sob story," I said trying to lighten up the mood. I know I told him the old story but I rather tell him this than the one with him being alive and with a different name and identity, all that drama doesn't need to be brought out to the light just yet.
he cheered up with the change of the topic "I'm Adrain Foster, 23 years old final year business studies student at the community college, Boston. I'm an only child, my parents say near the quarters of the forest department since they love nature..." he talked the entire way and the cheerfulness in his mood brought a genuine smile on my face.
"She said to meet at the bowling point," I said reading her text. the Mall was bigger than any other mall, they had everything that includes, a movie theater, bowling point, cafe, and many more. on our way to the bowling point, I saw a clothing store and checked out my outfit, I was not comfortable with the dress I'm wearing in a public place like this.
"Adrian, I'm gonna do a little shopping how about I meet you at the bowling point?" I asked waiting for his reply, he nodded and walked off.
After a quick pit stop at the store, I was now very comfortable in ankle jeans, full sleeves shirt, and sneakers. I feel much more like myself in these clothes now.
"Hey..." I said sitting on the bench where Nicole and Adrian were bowling with another guy I don't know of but looking at how Nicole is jumping at him seems like he is with her.
"Hey, where were you?" she asked me and I gave her a You-dare-ask-me look to which she smiled at me sheepishly. "sorry, the wrong question," she smiled

"I had a small pit stop to the clothing store since I could roam around the mall with a side split cocktail dress now, can I?" I taunted while ordering cocoa milkshake and french fries, I looked at the hot guy beside her "I don't think we have met? I'm Erika Price, Nicole's high school friend," I offered him my hand smiling and he accepted smiling back He tall maybe be 5'9, with curly hair, dark eyes, dark skin, and a nice smile. "Hi, I'm Miles Stuart, I'm sorry about last night it was my fault, actually we had a fight a couple of weeks ago and stopped talking but last night when I saw her all the feeling surfaced and we had to move away from people because what we were going to do was not legal in public yet," he laughed when Nicole hit his arm blushing embarrassingly

"It's ok, luckily I woke up in a nice stranger's house rather than a complete psychopath. so, all is good," I said mischievously still tiring to make her feel guilty. she whined like a spoilt brat on showing her mistake making me smile.

"How many times do I have to apologize for this," she cried out in frustration and we all laughed "By the Viper here is our very good friend and I trusted him to get you home safe which he did, thanks by the way," she said the last sentence to Adrian

I choked on my milkshake (stop that smile, you dirty people) and snorted "You call him that?" I asked wiping my mouth with the tissue.

both of them laughed "Yes when we heard his friend call him Viper we wouldn't let this opportunity slide," we laughed

We enjoyed the whole day talking, bowling, eating. it was a good day.

but then the Monday came and the hell broke loose,

remember the name of the company I worked yeah, the Price Enterprise. it was drowning I mean literary all the market shares were brought anonymously and the company was on the verge of collapse.

I went to the top floor of the building and greeted Rose she was the CEO's PA, I knocked at the door and was allowed in "Robert? Is everything ok?" I asked looking at his wrinkling face, he looked much older than he did last time I saw him.

"Erika my child, " he smiled at me "I'm fine, come sit down," he said gesturing to the empty chair opposite to him.

I sat on the chair and watched him "Are you sure you are ok? "I enquired again but he waved it off.

"I'm too old for this, I don't know how I'm gonna do this without Dimitri, he was exceptionally good with this and I'm not him," he spoke with so much pain in his voice that it brought tears to my eyes.

"Yeah, he was good," I said smiled at the faraway look on his face, he seemed to be recalling a happy moment with his grandson.

"I'm sorry for your loss my dear," he said

"I'm sorry for yours too," we smiled sadly at each other for a few minutes and then fell into silence "Did you find out about the buyer?" I asked spotting the elephant in the room.

"No, but the committee thinks it someone from Brazil," he said and I paled in my place

Brazil? Dimitri/Massimo is in Brazil

God! don't tell me he did this?

but the real question is why? why destroy the company you made? why hurt the people who raised him? why?

What are you planing Ex-Husband?

It's been a year since the downfall of the Price Enterprise company, piece by piece, shares by shares the business was at its last breath. the person suffering the most from this downfall was Robert Price. He looks tired, old, and helpless every time I meet him he looks older every passing second. he tried for a loan but the bank wouldn't sanction him one, he sorts out his friends and business partners but no one wants to invest in a drowning company. It's heartbreaking watching the most prestigious people crumble to the ground.

"Hey, you ready to go?" asked Adrian, yeah, the bartender Adrian. we are sort of best friends now, attached to the hips and he also works here at Price enterprise as an intern. The funny thing is even after telling him not to join my company he still insisted. I don't know why but his stubbornness is kind of a relief to me since I have a nagging feeling of loneliness in a deep part of my soul which thrived for attention.

"Yeah, let's go," I walked out with him towards the parking lot

"what do you want for dinner?" He asked me as we drove off in my car, we're kind of carpooling since his bike in the garage for servicing. well, that's what he told me but I know the truth, there have been some unusual things happening to me or around me, he has had a couple of accidents lately, be it mugging or hit and run or just bar fight.

"I'm carving Chinese," I smile at him while keeping an eye on the road, it's been a habit I always have an eye out on the road since the night of the accident.

"I know a great place," he said excitedly adding the address of the restaurant on the GPS, he is always full of energy and has a bright smile even at his worst he still smiles. he makes my heart flutter with feelings and warmth but I know it's not the flutter I crave.

We arrived at a small cozy old fashioned Chinese place, it had the typical Chinese outlook with bamboos and everything was in deep red.

"I know it's not much but they have the best Chinese in the city," he said nervously his cheeks colored with embarrassment

I chuckled at his anticks "I love it, it feels like home," I commented to which he let out a breath of relief.

we sat on the bamboo table and an Asian waiter came to take out the order, I ordered spicy shrimp and pad Thai noodles, Adrian chooses a simple Chinese platter. we ate in peace while making small talks here and there, Adrian did most of the good talking because I have an introverted personality which sucks at the times like these, Adrian being an extrovert took up all that load off of me and talked about his day as an intern and how his boss was making him do all the unrequited work.

I felt eyes on me, this was not the first time I've felt this, it is always there wherever I go. I glanced behind Adrian and saw a person in all black sitting at the far end of the restaurant. I have noticed him a few times but he was too close today.

"Can you excuse me for a minute? I need to use the bathroom," I asked him already standing up.

"Do you want me to come with you?" he asked while shoving a dumpling in his mouth.

I shook my head at him "it's ok, I'll be back," I walked towards the bathroom while crossing the mysterious person, he pretended to be engrossed in his meal but I doubt he even knows it's named.

I went inside the bathroom and waited for a couple of minutes, then exited and paid the bill and left for our car, Adrian was talking again, something about the bar where he still works. then I saw the man tailing us again
"turn here," I pulled Adrian into the isolated corner of the parking lot.
"Hey, what's up?" he asked alerted by my behavior
"We have a tail," I tell him hiding behind a pillar
The stalker lost our sight and walked ahead of us which gave me an advantage, I walked behind him and hit his leg, holding his arm, kicking him down on the ground and when he attempted to take out his gun, I smacked it out of his hand and took it, aiming at his head. all of this happened in a few seconds which scared the crap out of Adrian.
"What the hell? Erika, what the hell are you doing?" he panicked but I stared at the man
"Who are you?" I asked, "And why are you following us?" pointing the gun at him
"You're not gonna shoot me," mocked me, I took off the safety and shot at his leg he screamed out in pain like a motherfucker.
"I asked you a question and take off that mask?" I stared at him angrily, Adrian looked shell-shocked with what was going on.
he took off his mask, he is a typical white American with a tattoo all over his neck and piercings on his lips and eyebrow. "I'm just doing my job," he admitted wicking in pain as the blood streamed out of his leg.
"Who sent you?" I asked reloading the gun and aiming at his other leg
"I think you know him better than anyone," he replied indirectly avoiding my confrontation.

I stilled for a moment understanding the means of his vague words. "Why? " I asked he smiled creepily
"Why don't you ask him?" he laughed then winced in pain
"He is here?" I lowered the gun, looking at him shocked
"He was always here," he smiled and jumped at me for the gun but the sound of sirens had him stilled. the police arrived at the wrong time, Adrain pulled the gun out of my hand and threw it on the ground, the police arrested the stocker and took him away, he smiled oddly and screamed at me for one last time
"He is coming for you,"
Silence, deafening silence.
After the incident, we didn't speak with each other but I could hear the wheels turning in Adrain's head
"What was all that about?" Finally, the question left his mouth, surprisingly a person as loud as him The tone of his voice was quite calm but there were underlining fear and nervousness in his composure.
I sighed looking out the window and back at the road ahead
" I don't know that either "
" he knew you and you seemed to know who he was talking about, Erika, are you in some kind of trouble?" he asked looking worried for me which warmed my heart, it's been a while since someone was worried for me
"I not in trouble Adrian, it's just a ghost from the past coming back to haunt me, nothing to worry," I said and stopped at his apartment dropping him off
"No matter what I'll always be there for you," he said smiling at me and leaned closer to my face and stopped right in front of my face, our lips inches apart. I leaned away knowing the next action he sighed " one day, I hope you understand my feelings and reciprocate until then I'll be

waiting," he said then kissed my cheek before getting out of the car

I sighed and leaned my head on the steering wheel and groaned in frustration, I want to move on, I really, do but every time I try to kiss someone or try to initiate a move on someone, I back out at the last second. It's like my body doesn't want to reciprocate with my mind, every time Adrian leans down to kiss me I back out, I want to kiss him, be with him, he is a very nice guy and would keep me happy but he is not him, and unfortunately, I can't have both

Hating myself for what I have been doing to Adrian I drove back to my apartment, I had moved out of my mother's house since I don't want to burden her. I park my car in the basement parking lot and pressed 7 on the number plate on the side of the elevator door. I was too tired to greet the neighbors as they entered the elevator as well. I walked to my apartment door and opened it to be greeted with a small being wrapping themselves on my legs, that action brought a smile to my face

"Oscar, how are you baby, did you miss me?" I picked him and smoldered his face with kisses, he barked happily and wiggled in my arms. Oscar is a Labrador retriever, a gift from my friend Nicole as a housewarming present.

As I poured Oscar's food into his bowl I noticed something on the coffee table, there was a bouquet and there was a note along with it. I hesitated before picking it up and it said 'Nice Dog'

I didn't sleep a wink last night and the tiredness was taking its toll on me. The next morning I stepped inside the Price building and was met with chaos. Media was everywhere and they were crowding the lobby, security was doubled with the number of people trying to get into the main

building.
"Mrs. Price?" One of the reporters yelled pointing her mike and camera towards me. Everyone must have heard her because in less than a second I was surrounded by flashes of camera and mikes shoved in my face.
"Did you know this was going to happen!"
"Were you a part of this conspiracy too?"
"Will The Price Enterprise succubus into nothing "
"Did you know Mr. Dimitri Price faked his own death?"
The last question startled me and I started shocked at the reporter incomplete astonishment
"What?" I inquired
The security got to me to safety before they bombard me with more questions
I had to know what happened within the course of 24 hours that has completely turned the tables
"Robert?" I called out as I entered his cabin and he was sitting on his chair with his head in his hands.
"Did you know?" He whispered, I barely heard it
"What?" I asked again
"Did you know" he yelled angrily standing up from his chair
"I don't- I don't understand," I said calmly
"Did you know he was alive?" He banged his wrinkled hand on the glass table, I winced at the loud noise
I stayed silent looking at the wooden flooring
"Why? Why didn't you tell me?" He flung the phone off the table furiously
"He- I" I stuttered
"And why would he buy his own company?" He ran his hand in his salt and pepper hair extremely stressed
"What? I didn't know that?" I said hesitated
"Yeah, he bought this company as well as all our assets, we

are practically bankrupted and there is nothing I can do" he sighed "but why is he doing this? All of this us his, anyways "

I stayed silent and didn't say anything because I didn't really know anything about this.

And there was only one person who can answer all these questions, and it's time to face my demons

Time to face Massimo Torricelli

"Hello?"

"I need to see Massimo" I demand pacing around my office running my hand through my hair

"What- how did you get this number?" Peter asked confused probably looking at his phone

"That's not important, I need to talk to him," I say with a hint of desperation in my voice but I don't let it show

"I'm not his bitch, I don't know where he is," he said

" You are, just tell him I want to meet" with that I hang up

After I met with Robert, I had no idea what was going on, his actions towards the company clearly explain that he is not back for me. But why the hell would he attack his own company, I mean he was the main reason the company has had its glory but now it was down into crumbles.

I sigh in frustration and take a deep breath, hoping it would calm my racing heart. I started thinking about the time when I was at his house in Rio. He told me about his family, he was not actually a Price, if he was not Robert's grandson then why pretend? Is it something else? What am I missing? All these questions were wearing me out. So, after a lot of self-arguments, I focused on getting some work done, glancing at my table a thought crossed over my mind that maybe I should start packing, maybe I will b removed from

my job?
Letting out some frustrating groan I sit on my couch and browse through my emails, decided to get pending work done I drown in it.
I was too deep into my work that I didn't realize what time it was until my PA came knocking down my door. Bidding goodbyes and good nights I leave.
I kept looking at my phone for Peter's call or a text assuring me that Massimo is ready to meet, or at least talk. Sighing in disappointment I open the door of my apartment and was met with silence
"Oscar? Baby where are you?" I ask while taking off my heels and turned the lights on
I squeak in a very un-ladylike surprise to see Massimo sitting on my couch with My Oscar purring like a cat in his lap.
I place my hand on my racing heart trying to calm down. I lean on the door and watch him staring at me like some kind of meal.
"I see you got my message, looks like he is your bitch after all," I say placing my keys in the bowl and sat across from him, I was too aware of his intense stare
I cleared my throat nervously 7 years and this guy still has me shivering nervously " I - 'm sure you are wondering why I wanted to see you" I didn't get a reply but his eyes say I have his attention
I stared at him a little not much has changed during the past year, he looks dashing as ever in his intense black suit and white undershirt his dark hair perfectly styled, I gulp nervously suddenly feeling too dry in my throat. My actions don't go unnoticed by him more over his eyes turned a darker shade.
"What do you want Erica?" He asked with his deep voice, a

shiver went down my back only he has the power to do that to me with just his voice.
I lick my dry lips almost forgetting my main purpose of inviting him over
"It's about The price enterprise?" I say more like a question.
He raised his dark brow in question
"What about it?" He asked patting Oscar while sitting up straighter
"I saw Robert today" I sighed recalling his devastated expression " He looked so broken Dimitri" the name slipped out. His expression turned pissed and his hands turned to fists
"I'm sorry, old habits I guess" I cough awkwardly
"That was not a question, Erika, " he said impatiently
"Why are you doing this? The company was already yours" I asked running my hand through my locks
"That's got nothing to do with you" he dismissed my question looking around my apartment with interest then stood up to look around and touched things
"They are my Family Massimo, so are yours," I say angry with his arrogant behavior
He scoffed " they are not my family, they are not your family either not anymore," he said holding a photo frame of me and my mother
"They might not be my family but they raised you, fed you, clothed you, they educated you" he ignored my rant and continue to look around he slowly reached my bedroom and I followed him
"Massimo, I'm talking to you" I yell at him frustrated with his stupid behavior
(Contains mild mature scenes)
He turned around stalking towards me and trapped me

between him and my bedroom wall. He placed his arms on either side of me, his face was inches away from mine
"Say it again," he whispered, his warm minty breath on my face making me feel things I'm not supposed to
"What?" I asked breathlessly with his proximity my mind was jumbled
"My name, say my name" he whispered, his face getting closer if it was possible
His name was at the tip of my tongue but flashes of what he has done to me and his family got me to get my shit together and pushed him off of me. He stumbled completely surprised by my actions
"No, you don't get to do that. You divorced me, left me, you- you " my words were jumbled, it was too overwhelming for me to say anything
He closed the distance between us and smashed his lips on mine, the sensation was completely uncalled for but I was not sure if I liked this or not.
He moved his amazingly soft lips online and wrapped his arm around my waist and pulled me impossibly closer to his hard body. I gave up the fight between pushing him away or pulling him closer, I moved my lips mimicking his actions, and wrapped his arms around his neck to pull him closer, which encourages him to deepen the kiss, he licked my bottom lip for entrance which got me shivering. I opened my mouth for him, his luscious tongue entered my awaiting mouth, he pulled me closer again, I felt every curve, every muscle on his body through his silk shirt.
His tongue fought mine for dominance which he won of course, with my lack of any kind of experience in this field, he placed his other hand on my head and pulled my hair receiving a gasp from me. He trailed his sinful lips down my

neck and bit down on my collar bone, which had been losing my footing. He held my butts and whispered in my ear "jump " I obeyed him like a silly little girl and jumped on him, wrapping my legs around his waist. He pulled us towards my bed all while kissing me like there was no tomorrow

He dropped us on the bed, the pencil skirt that I wore was too easy to access. He settled between my legs and kissed my lips with too much pressure which had me seeing stars. He pulled away that had me whimper he chuckled softly then pulled off his more blase with so much urgency, he pulled the buttons on his shirt without care and threw it off somewhere in the room. He is too good looking for this world, he paused when he saw me admiring his god gifted body, his broad shoulders, his arms, his eight packs were so unreal, I had a hard time believing a person with this of the body even existed, the sexiest part was the trail of hair leading down his perfect v line had me uncomfortable in my own skin in a very good way

He leaned down kissing my lips and pulling my hair, I moved my hands on his well-defined body, tracing every line, peck, and pattern on his skin. But when his hand found a way under my shirt, I went completely liquid. His hard warm hand feeling my smooth skin, rubbing slow circles. Maybe the fabric of my dress shirt was too much for him that had him ripping my shirt off of me, my eyes widened surprised by his actions. He paused all his actions and pulled away for a little to admire the sight before him. I blushed terribly due to the amount of lust in his eyes, eyeing my lacy black lingerie bra. He growled low in his throat " beautiful" he said before kissing down the path between my cleavage. I gasped with this new sensation, the wetness between my legs was too overwhelming, I have never felt anything like this before. It was too intense

His hands were near my breasts, just before he could fondle with them his phone rang in his pants, he ignored the first time and continued cherishing my body but then my phone rang, he growled in frustration and stood up. His frustrated expression had me giggling like a schoolgirl. He pecked my lips one last time and said "this is not over"

He pulled out his phone and walked out of the bedroom, the yelling and growling were too loud but then he hung up and came back inside the room. I hadn't moved an inch from my position, I was breathing heavily, my heart was pounding in my ears and the adrenaline rush was wearing off too quickly

He stood over me for a minute admiringly then leaned down to give me a soul-burning kiss that has my toes curling. "I'll be back," he said kissing my forehead then moved to pick his ruined shirt and walked away.

I took a minute to gather myself when the front door shut with a soft thud. I looked at my ripped shirt and ran my fingers on the sensitive parts of my neck and felt the bruises of his harsh lips. I laid back on the bed and groaned

"What the fuck just happened"

With the sudden change of events, last night's sleep didn't come to me there was so much passion between us which was never there before, five years with him and we have never done anything else not even close to kissing. Every time I tried to kiss him he would push me away but this time it was the how initiated the kiss.

I could still feel him on my skin, his warm minty breath, his sinful lips, and his hands. God! Those hands

Shaking away those memories I get up from my bed and take a much-needed shower. Super hot water tracing down my skin washing away last night's sin. I dress up for another day of chaos called Massimo Torricelli

I got to the Price Enterprise main building and was surprised to see what was going on. The name on the building was being taken down the logo was replaced with a giant M&T

I stare wide-eyed with disbelief and walk inside the building, Every fucking thing was either replaced or changed completely. All the staff members were walking around packing their belongings in a single box.

"Alessandra, what's going on?" I ask one of our senior employees as she was rushing around almost in tears

"Oh, Ms. Black you don't know? Last night all of us got our termination letter emailed and we were asked to gather our belongings today, " her happy smile was betrayed with traitorous tears. I pulled her into a hug and she let out a sad sob

This was too much he can't do this to these hardworking employees. "I'll talk to him, please don't cry," I wipe her tears giving her a reassuring smile.

As I walked deeper into the building, everywhere I look I see people either packing or new people settling down. I stomp on my high heels and stalked towards the CEO cabin. I had a hunch I might find him there.

Robert's PA was at her desk outside the CEO cabin, her smile calmed me a little but the tears on Alessandra's face brought back the fury in me.

I didn't knock and barged into the room, there seemed to be a meeting going on Every head in the room turned to me but mine was stuck to the root of this problem, Massimo

stared at me like he was expecting my reaction
I glared at him with hate and disgust. I can't believe it's the same person from last night
"If you excuse us please," he kicked them out without taking his eyes off of me.
The four of them were new and a woman in a very reveling formal dress shirt gave me sting eyes, I scoff inwardly 'bitch, you can have him'
"Please have a seat, Ms. Black," he gestured towards the chair opposite to his
I snort at him and walk directly to face him and place my hands on the glass table and glare daggers at his smug little face.
"What do you think you're doing?" I ask him not to break eye contact, I agree his deep grey eyes were calling out to me. Dominating me into submission " And where is Robert? Why the hell are you termination good people without any good reason?" I almost scream in his face.
His non-responsive face was making me pull out my hair in frustration
"I own this Company, Ms. Black, Robert is retired from his position and for the terminated employees. I do have a reason and that is they are not capable of working in my company," he stands up and walks towards me, making me stumble back because of his intimidating strides.
He stood in front of me and cornered me between him and his glass table. I don't know how I keep ending up in this position. The dark suit he wore was doing things to me and his Armani perfume mixed with his own unique scent was turning my brain into mush.
I compose myself and move out of his hold and take a deep breath. I started to walk away from him when he grabbed

my wrist and pulled my back.
"Where are going?" He asks with his deep voice, as my back was on his front I could feel the vibration of his words.
I gulp nervously "going to pack, of course, I don't see no purpose of me being around," I say but don't move
He leaves my wrist but wrap his arm around my waist and pulled me impossibly closer to his hard body, he takes a deep whiff on my hair and groans with pleasure
"You always smell so divine" he mutters tracing his nose down the length of my neck. I quiver in my spot with intense pleasure I let out a very low moan which broke down the spell on him. He pulled away from me but didn't let go in fact he turned me around and pushed me on the table and held my waist and sat me down on it.
He grabbed my hair and pulled my lips into a bruising kiss. He moved my legs apart and settled between them, luckily I wore my trousers, which were easier to access. He left my hair but placed his large hands on my ass and pulled me tighter molding my body into his. He moved his lips on me with so much hunger it made me shiver with delight.
I wrapped my hands on his back pulling him closer, I pulled at his hair, scratched his back, and did everything I could to keep him where he was.
He groaned in my mouth as I pulled his hair, his hands moved from my back to my ass and squeeze them like there was tomorrow
His kiss was turning me into a hot mess, the way his tongue played with mine was driving me crazy. His tongue was tracing every nook and cranny of my mouth. I gasped in surprise when his hands found their way underneath my shirt, he fumbled with the clasp of my bra trying to undo it. That's where my common sense came back to me and I

pushed him away from me.
I stared at him breathing heavily, running my hands down my hair. He tried to move closer to me again but I placed my hand on his chest halting him. He was exhaling deeply too but the predator look on his face was turning me on beyond everything. Every fiber in my body was protesting against me for stopping him from continuing.
"Why does every conversation end up with us pulling off each other's clothes?" I ask him chuckling nervously
He holds my hand on his chest and moves closer to me. He leans connecting our foreheads and smiled "because I finally got you all to myself and this time I'm not letting you go,"

He leaned down to kiss me again but there was a knock on the door that earned a groan of annoyance from him and a giggle from me. He pecked my lips for the last time and pulled away winking playfully
As he walked to sit in his seat I jumped down from the table and straighten my messy clothes.
"Come in," he said in a powerful voice that did things to me, I redden shyly when he keeps looking at me with the same look.
The same woman from before entered into the office, she looked annoyed and disgusted when she glared at my messy appearance
"I'll go get my things then, " I announced and was about to leave but his words stopped me.
"No, You're not packing your things," he notified me before looking at the intruder for an explanation
"Why not ?" I asked "all of my people are " I answered back
"Because you are not fired, Ms. Black," he said dismissively, I raised my eyebrow in a challenge

"I want my team back if I'm staying, if not then goodbye, Mr. Torricelli, " I nod my head at both of them and leave with powerful strides

I greet people on my way to the fourth floor to my office and opened my office door but the sight of some guy settling down and moving things startling me in my spot.

"hmm... excuse me what do you think you're doing?" I asked him walking to stand across him stopping him from whatever that he was doing in MY office.

"oh, you must be Ms. Black, I'm Harry Stewart nice to meet you," he came forward and held out his hand for me to shake, I, on the other hand, stood starstruck at what the hell was going on. he pulled his hand away embarrassed with my rude behavior "one moment please," he lifts his index finger, he walked around my table and pulled out an access card handing it to me, I raised an eyebrow

"I was asked to deliver this to you," he smiles nervously as he offers me the access card

I look at him suspiciously but take the card nonetheless. My name was written on the card as well as a bar code. "What is this?" I ask Harry, he scratches the back of his neck and answer

"You are supposed to move in on the 14th, floor. Boss's order, " he says not meeting my eyes.

I spare the poor man as he was already shaking in his boots and decided to do what he said. I walked out of my old room without any of my stuff because there wasn't any and pressed the 14th floor on the elevator, I waited to go from the 5th to 14th floor

When I walked out of the door, there were only two doors on this floor which had me scowling I walk to the first door but it was a conference room then I walked to the second

door there was an access card reader. I swiped my card and opened the door.
It is a very fancy well-furnished office there were walls made completely out of glass and the table was too. There are a very fluffy couch and a very nice boss chair. What caught my attention was the nameplate on the table
"Vice President, " I read out loud not believing my eyes, I kept blinking making sure I was seeing right.
"Erika Black, Vice President, " I hadn't noticed Massimo walking in. I turned to face him, he was leaning on the doorway looking all smug and happy "has a nice ring to it, right?" He said walking closer to me
I stammered" I- I don't know what to say" I admitted not completely over this shocking revelation
He chuckled standing in front of me, he held my shoulders and pulled me closer

And I was right about his plan being bigger than all of us because later that week, The Price Mansion was being vacated, like completely thrown out, I have no idea what was going on but this was too for me to watch
"what the hell is wrong with you?" I yelled at him with so much anger that his PA flinched, he sighed tiredly, like he was expecting my outburst.
"Excuse us, " he told his PA and walked towards me, he yanks on my arm and pulls me out of the room. He glares at me when we are pulled into an empty conference room.
"Who do you think you are? Huh, barging into my office, as you own it, I'm done with your ungrateful ass of an attitude, " he screamed in my face, his face was furious and the veins on his face were making itself known.
I was stunned by his outburst and was slightly afraid of him,

I didn't say anything I wanted to make sure he spoke his anger out before I add gasoline, to this fire.
"You had no right to kick your own grandparents out of their own house" I yelled back with the same kind of fury
He pulled me closer "what I do with them is none of your concerns, and what they are to me is my problem, not yours" he pushed me away with a jerk "stay away, you are not a Price any more. know your limits or you will be removed the same way they are, " with that he walked out of the conference room
I stood there comprehending what the fuck just happened, the reality of the situation drowned down at me, and his words no matter how vicious but what he said was right, I have no right to interfere in their business. I was in a contract relationship with him and it ended with a divorce but with my experience and emotions I share with the family, is not something I could neglect
I drove back to the Price mansion and see movers moving things left and right, Robert was on a phone call talking aggressively, whereas Adaline was sitting on a recliner sipping wine from her glass.

"Adaline, how are you? I'm so sorry this is happening," I tell her as I sit across from her and hold her unoccupied hand, she raised her head to look at her and snarled.
she ripped her hand out of my grasp and stood from her seat " how am I? how dare you come into this house and ask about my wellbeing? you wretched bitch," she tilts her wine glass on my head. Red wine poured down on me, sinking into my white dress shirt as it completely drenches my hair with the alcoholic beverage, I gasp in shock at her expected behavior. " get the hell away from me and my

family!" she screamed "everything was so good until you came along, my baby pretended to be dead so get rid of you, and now he won't even look at me, this is all your fault he is like this because of you. you did this," she ended up crying as she falls on the floor weeping into tears. it took me a moment to gather myself into realizing what had happened Robert saw the whole thing and came running to help his weeping wife, he held her close and look at me " I think it's better if you leave now," he looked at me with the same look of accusation he bore not so long ago.

Defeated I leave the mansion and drove back home, I jump into the shower first and scrub the remnants of the expensive red wine off my body, I don't go back to the office but take care of things from home. I tried to busy myself with work so, I couldn't think of the incident that took place today, I sigh placing my laptop on the coffee table and look at the ceiling and recall all the memories of the past six years of my life, all of those include unwanted stress and fake relationship.

"Maybe it's time to move on, maybe I need some me time," I say out loud and nod to myself, I pull out my phone from my bag and order a huge jumbo size pepperoni pizza with lots of cheez, but for beverage, I had to go to the nearby store, because my kind of beverage was vodka. the order would be here in 20 minutes so it was enough time for me to buy vodka. I change into some jeans and a t-shirt and grab my wallet.

the store was just a block away so I didn't take my car, a nice walk gave me some time to explore my surroundings. as it was just 6 in the evening, all the children were playing, some people were walking their dog which reminded me to do the same tomorrow morning. I grab a trolley and explore my options, it also reminded me to get some groceries as well. I put everything I could carry back with me on foot and took two bottles of virgin vodka to checkout. as I neared my apartment complex, I see the pizza delivery boy waiting outside the main door, I had to buzz him in.

"Hey, is that for apartment 312?" I ask the pizza boy, he stared at me for a second like in a trance but snapped out before checking the order details, nodded holding out the pizza but hesitated due to too many bags in my hands. "do you mind helping me carry the pizza to my apartment?" I ask politely.

"Yeah, sure," he said I murmured thanks and buzzed us both in, we spoke in the elevator till we reached my floor. he told me his name was Blake and he was still in high school and was helping his uncle with a part-time job. when we got out of the elevator there was someone at my door waiting.

"Can I help you?" I asked the person whose back was towards me, he turned around he was Adrian. he looked at Blake in question but smiled when we approached him

"I was just checking in because you didn't up at work today," he smiled " here let me get that," he pulled the groceries bag out of my hands and looked at Blake

"Oh, this my Blake he is here to deliver my pizza," I said taking the large pizza box from his hands, Adrian put his hand in his pocket to pull out the cash when I told him I've already paid. Blake left after that and I let Adrian into my house.

"did you had dinner," I asked him while separating vodka bottles from the groceries, he looked at the bottles amused

"Anything special today?" he asked helping me store the vegetables into the fridge

"Yeah, something like that," and yes, it was. today was special because I havrealizeded my worth and it's time to move on from my old and complicated life
"then, how about some horror movies," he said excitedly and I laughed "bring it on," I hope my life takes a right turn from now on.

The very next morning I had written a long and very resourceful resignation letter and I had emailed it to the source of my unhappiness, the CEO of the M&T chain of companies.
I had ignored all of his urgent calls and texts, his voicemails begged to differ that he might be happy to know I dropped his ass flat on the pavement. Doesn't matter if he is happy or not, I won't let him play with my life like some board game.
I inhale a deeply encouraging and brave breath to get out of the car and walk towards the M&T building the bane of my existence
I smile at everyone on my way towards my ex-office and for the last time slide in my access card. On entering the room was just the way I left it, quickly I gather up my stuff and put it in a single box, I know it's a coward way out but I'm not ashamed of it. If I don't do it now I can never have the courage to do it again.
I look at the room one more time and drop the key card on the table and leave, this time for good. I walk to the elevator and press to go down to the parking lot, the door was about to be closed when a hand stopped it and much to my dismay it was just the PA, I smile forcefully and stood there till we hit the ground, I leave the building and surprisingly, I didn't come around any kind of drama, no yelling, no breaking of

things, no pushing on the wall and kissing nothing it was like he was finally letting me go. I get into my car and just stay there thinking, imagining, something he could do to stop me, but nothing as if I didn't matter to him like I thought I would. Funny enough I'm not angry, disappointed, definitely but not angry

It's like deep down I knew he didn't love me the way I did, we'll he can screw himself for all I care because I'm done.

I drove off, the building looked smaller and smaller as I drove away, it's like a huge weight had lifted off of me and I can finally breathe again.

Obviously, I didn't leave my apartment because I didn't think of leaving the city just yet but I'll think of something, I have enough in the savings to go on a couple of months without a job.

The first thing I did was call up Nicole and gather up some of our friends for a get-together or a small party. Well at least I thought I did but I ended up going to the sexiest club in the city and got shit faced drunk with only Nicole because both of us didn't need other people to celebrate my walk away

Nicole laughed at me drunk as hell herself too "your shit faced, " she giggled crazily

I giggled twice as hard "no, your shit faced" we both doubled over laughing we look over the bartender "Mr. Bartender, two more shots, please" I order smiling, at him all drunk

I look over Nicole "he is such an asshole, I mean he didn't even try to stop me, " I exclaim upset, she nods not getting a single word "I mean he left me twice" I show her my two fingers "twice, and I went out to find him, and that motherfucker didn't really stop me or call me or break down my front door and beg me to come back, " I ramble again and again "you know what I should call him, " I say wicked She sobers up a little "no, no Erika that's a bad idea, " she tries to reach for my phone but I move away

"Yes, yes it's a very good idea, I should call him and trash talk to him and get all that frustration out " I hit the call option and wait for him to pick up

"Hello, " he said his voice neutral and seductive

"Listen here you piece of shit, " I start getting out of my seat to stand and scream into the phone

"Erika?" He asked certainly shocked by my statement

"Yes, it's me you son of a bitch, you are such an asshole, you left me twice TWICE! And I still came looking for you, searching for your sorry ass and you didn't stop me" I cry at the end of my angry rant, the other side of the line was silent I almost hung up thinking he was gone but his breathing was audible so at least he was listening

"You... you... you didn't even try to stop, pull me closer slam me to the wall and convince me with a mind-blowing kiss and beg me to stay, Six years Dimitri, six-fucking-years, and nothing, I mean nothing to you, you bastard I hope you did alone and regret when you watch me get married, have kids and grow old with a person who is gonna love me so much that you can't even imagine, I hate you, I fucking hate you, " with that, I hang up sobbing into the floor completely heartbroken, Nicole sat beside me holding me closer and rocking me back and forth as I sobbed into her chest like a baby

I don't remember much but I wake up on the softest best with an amazing view of huge windows and a white royal suite, with a balcony facing the cities view. I looked at my right and found snoring, cake faced, completely smashed

Nicole and smile
For the last time, I think I'm going to be Okay

It's been a couple of months since I big move on and I have been excellent, I've discovered that I love being by myself and I'm treating my dog better, I run a lot, joined a yoga class, meditation, and cooking.
It has been a nice couple of days until I find Oliver, Dimitri/ Massimo's cousin brother, knocking on my door.
"Hey, " he said nervously I smiled
"Hey, " I pull him into a hug, "oh, my god, how are you, " I said pulling away "come in, "
He smiled politely "nice house, it would have been easier to find you if you didn't ghost me, " he says accusation clear in his eyes.
I was my hand in defense, we sat on the couch side by side " guilty, I'm just trying to move on, you know to find myself, " he smiled sadly at me, he knows that the pity is the last thing I need
"Enough about me, tell me about you? How are you? And how's your boyfriend Pete?" I ask standing up to get some coffee
He followed me into the kitchen, " I've been better, life's good and Pete is not my boyfriend anymore, " I stopped what I was doing and watch him
I hold the coffee pot "should I get a beer instead?" I ask and he laughs
"No, no he is not my boyfriend anymore because" he raised his left hand and showed me his ring "he is now my fiancee, " I keep the pot of coffee on the counter and squeak excitedly
"Oh my god, seriously" I jump on him into a fierce hug "I'm

so happy for you" we laugh as he swings me around, we stop before anyone of us falls down
"Yeah, I'm happy for myself, too," he said smiling lovingly looking at his finger, I smile too happy for him
"Tell me everything, " I say as I pull him towards the couch with coffee cups in our hands, "who proposed who? "
He smiled at the memory "I had a plan in mind when we went to his favorite beach in Miami, a candlelight dinner on the sand, with the sunset and all with me wearing a white tux, on my knees, a very awkward and long heartfelt speech, " he chuckled lightly, I smiled at his behavior, deeply in love. What a wonderful feeling it is.
"So, that didn't happen?" I asked curiously
"No, it was going as planned till the dinner but guess we had the same idea because he too got on his knee and pulled out a ring" I 'aww' at his cute little blushing face
"I'm seriously very happy this happened to you, you deserve this" we smiled at each other
I cough awkwardly "ok, now the ice breaker" he laughed silly
"Yeah, they know, " see that his parents being from a very conservative family they didn't like homosexuals, which had delayed Oliver to come out to them.
"And" I push for more details
He shrugged, "I don't care if they approve of my marriage or not, and since they don't have their precious status in the society anymore, they can't bully me into not marrying the love of my life" he declares proudly but there is sadness behind the strong facade, I didn't push it much
"Status?" I ask sipping my coffee
"Yeah, all the wealth and dignity they had was ripped away from them when former Dimitri Price and now Massimo

Torricelli, he took everything and I mean everything the restaurants, their houses, cars business, everything. " he stops with a faraway look in his eyes

We sit quietly for a while "ok, enough about them now when is the wedding?" I ask excitedly

He gets his smile back " next week, " he smiles sheepishly "Greece, you're going to love it there" I don't say anything " you are coming right? I need my family, by my side" he holds my hand in his

I tear up a bit "of course I will be there, I wouldn't miss it for the world" we smiled and hugged the shit out of each other

We spent the whole day talking and discussing his wedding, he was so excited to plan the whole thing out and especially in a city like Greece

"I'm so happy it isn't in Paris, it would be so cliche, " I say and he laughs at that

"Trust me, Pete would kill me if we chose Paris, because he said and I quote 'Paris is overrated '" we laugh hearty and spend the rest of the day catching up on things we missed, then we came across the topic

"I heard about what Adaline did, I'm sorry " he apologized on her behalf, I waved it off, that wine incident was too old for me.

"It's not your fault, " I mumble

"I just don't understand why he did it though," he said confused I shrug not caring "you're not curious?" He asked

"I stopped asking questions when they stopped seeing me as a person, I mean I'm not the one who did it but everyone thinks it was my fault so I stopped caring " I shrug again.

"I'm sorry about him, I know you loved him a lot" he smiled sadly at me

"Yeah, sometimes love is not enough, " that we dismiss the conversation like it never happened and went back to his wedding, and apparently there still needs to be a bachelor party
I'm gonna call Nicole, again

So, here we are at New York's richest and most amazing gay club for Oliver's bachelor party.
"This is crazy, " Oliver chuckled looking at the male strippers who were swinging his barely cover crotch in his face. I laughed at his expression of sexual torture
We were dressed as strippers too, I had my long dark hair in a high ponytail with a braid and my costume was a leather bra and tight leather pants with high boots, and a little touch of sin a whip
Oliver and his work friends we're wearing leather pants, with Cowboy hats and an open jacket
Nicole was obviously wearing a sexy nun costume with an extra messy makeup
"Body shots?" Nicole asked mischievously looking at this sexy naked guy on the body shots table, all of Oliver's friends and colleagues laughed enjoying Oliver's embarrassment, he held his face with his hands blushing red
We pushed Oliver at the slab, the guy looked eager to serve the sexy doctor. We basically pushed his head till it was face to face with the belly button on a very naked man. He Chickens out at the last minute and runs into my arms embarrassed
We laugh at him and let him be, then we took the part in the stage area where there were dancing poles, with extremely flexible bodies.
There was another group of people who were louder than

us, and surprisingly it was Pete and his friends, he was getting a very hot lap dance from a very sexy guy.
I jabbed Oliver in the ribs to get his attention, the smile on his face brightened up but slowly faded when he saw Pete enjoying the attention of the stranger. For a second I thought I shouldn't have done that but surprisingly Oliver got on the stage and politely, asked the dance to move. Peter's famine features came in handy with the way he moved his body. He slowly moved his body up and down around the pole with seductive twerk that got Pete attention, the color escaped his face when he saw Oliver, he pushed the dancer out of his lap and got up to walk towards his fiancee
Oliver's sensual moves had caught a lot of people's attention and that got Pete to speed walk towards the stage, by that time he got to him, Oliver had now proceeded to shed his clothes and before he could undo his pants, Pete picked him up and threw him like a sack of potatoes on his shoulders, we cheered at them as he walked away to God knows where to, probably to punish his naughty fiancee
We laughed and got back to have fun around the club knowing them they are gonna take their sweet time
"Erika?" A familiar voice called out my name and unexpectedly it was Adrian, we hadn't invited him because he was busy during the weekend
"Adrian, hey" I side hugged him when he got closer. "What are you doing here?"
He smiled and gestured at the group of friends that sat with Pete "I was invited to my best friend's brother's bachelors party" I nodded understanding "you wanna dance?" He asked I nodded gulping down my last shot, I let him drag me to the middle of the dance floor, he held my waist and

pulled me closer

I didn't feel any butterflies other than the vibration of the loud music, he did his best to move his body against mine but my body refused to react the way it was supposed to with a hot guy. I excuse myself for a second and move toward the bar to get another drink.

"Rough night?" Asked the sexy half-naked bartender as he poured my shot

"Rough life, actually, " I finish the shot then moved away from the crowd for a breather, I let a breath as I stood near an open window. "Why am I like this?" I ask myself

Here I was at a gay club witnessing the most important day in my friend's life and I'm wearing the most sluty outfit I have ever worn and I'm still standing far away from the interesting crowd. Slowly my friend keeps disappearing with their flavors of the night, not that there were just men here there were women too, and lucky for my group they were also interested

I text Nicole and Oliver that I was going back to the hotel we book for losers who didn't get a hot date for the night.

I sigh and walk out of the club to our limo, "I would like to go back to the hotel, please" I say to the driver, he didn't say much but started driving, I watch the streets as we drive off but I sobered up when he didn't turn to the block where we were supposed to turn.

"Hello, sorry but you missed the turn," I say when no heed, I panic a little and "excuse me I'm talking to you, I said you missed a turn, you know what, why don't you just stop, ok, " I say trying to push the door but he locked them

"Stop, I said stop" I screamed started banging on the windows and his seat but he didn't budge

And then he turned "I know, we're not going to the hotel"

it was Massimo with a heated look in his eyes
This can't be good

Massimo was driving me somewhere, it wasn't like I was obediently sat still while he drove off to some fantasyland, no I did everything I could do to open the door or possibly a window but the limo didn't budge.
"We're here, " he announced like it was very normal to kidnap someone again of their will and hold them, hostage. I ignored him, he came around my door and pulled it open. I tried pushing him and running but no a wail he was too strong
He pulled me by my waist and threw me on his shoulder like no big deal. I punched his back and kept kicking him but it was extremely depressing to say that he probably didn't even feel it. Giving up I observed my surroundings and to my surprise, it was our house, the house he got me when we were married
The memories in this house were too much, this is the place I realized that I was head over heels in love with him and he wasn't.
He opened the door and walked inside with me handing over his shoulder. He threw me on the couch, I took my chance and ran to the door and tried opening it but the asshole had the doors locked, I could decode the locks but it could take some time and the way he was watching me amused I knew my chances of getting out were next to zero. I groaned in frustration and walked to sit on the couch, he walked towards the kitchen and yelled "drinks?" I followed him and crossed my arms
"Why am I here, Massimo?" I asked he pushed around the fridge to pull out a bottle of wine, he pours our drinks and

came towards me, he offered me a glass which I declined/ignored his eyes fell over my hands and his eyes turned a darker shade of grey

I look over myself and blush deep red with embarrassment and let my hands fall to my sides. I clear my throat to get his attention from my breasts

"We need to talk about that phone call" he simply says sipping wine

I huff " a little too late don't you think?" I lean on the wall to have a better look at his face

He gulps down his wine and places the glass on the kitchen counter and walks towards me losing his tie and unbuttoning his blazer and getting rid of it, he started to uncuff his shirt and rolled it on his arms. That single action had me so hot and bothered not even men in leather pants had that effect on me. He did all that without losing eye contact, the tiny smirk on his face said that he noticed my reaction to his striping session.

" I know and I'm sorry I couldn't reach you after that, but I'm here now and this time I'm going to make it right, " that he was right in front of me and I was engulfed with his sexy musky sent that blurred my thoughts

"And how are you going to do that?" The liquor in me was taking its effect and my intense desire to be with him was overpowering my sane mind.

"I have a lot of ways, it's better if I show you, " he leaned in and kissed me with so much passion that turned my insides into a puddle

MATURE CONTENT

"I'm sorry, " he murmured, and before I could reply his lips were back on mine. He kissed me with so much force, I wrapped my arms around his neck and pulled him closer.

His hands moved on my body expertly, feeling every dip and curve then settled down on my ass squeezing and fondling with them like they were some squeaking toy.
I gasped erotically as his lips moved down my neck kissing and biting on his way. "Jump" he whispered in my ear huskily and sucking the earlobe it had me shivering in pleasure, I did as he asked and wrapped my legs around his waist, he pulled me away from the wall while kissing the hell out of me. He moved expertly into the direction of our bedroom and closed the door, his smooth lips on my were devouring my mouth.
He threw me on the plush bed, I bounced on it. I watch him as he ripped his dress shirt and threw it on somewhere in the room then came back to me with double the urgency and double the pleasure.
I sat up and got rid of my leather top, and luckily I wasn't weren't a bra that got his eyes to turn darker with lust. He pushed on my back and kissed my lips, his hands went to my breasts squeezing them. He ran his finger over my right nip making it hard in the process. My breath hitched with the shot of pleasure that went through my body, I was literally seeing stars. His lips slowly descended my neck to my breasts, I saw him move and he didn't take his eyes off of me, he flicked my nip before taking it in his mouth and sucking the taut pink blossom, I gasped contentment.
He took it as an encouragement and did the same with my other nip, his warm breath hit my nip making it hard before diving to take it in his mouth, his hand cupped my other breast and kept it busy. I was withering in my place, my fingers were scratching and pulling on his hair, he took my hands and placed them above my head "keep them here, " the order in his voice was clear as daylight.

I grabbed the wooden handle on the bed and closed my eyes feeling his warm mouth abusing my nipples, his hands slowly moved downwards and stopped at the waistline of my leather pants. I opened my eyes as he was already looking at me with an intense look, I knew that look he was asking for permission to carry on.
Should I? Or maybe I should stop him now before it got out of hand. The continuous conflict in my mind was turning me sober. I closed my eyes for a second and I knew my answer
Then I nodded

My permission was all he needed before he pulled my pants down along with my seamless underwear, I thank Nicole internally for forcing me to wear matching underwear.
He kissed on hot skin from my belly button to the front of my heat. He pulled away from my heat to stare at it, his intense look makes me press my legs together but he growled sexually before pulling my legs apart and settling them down on his shoulders, he eagerly sucked on my clit like he was starving from a decade.
Pleasure shot through my body, the blood in my veins was rushing so fast to my heart that he might explode any minute now. My grip on the bed handle was so hard that my knuckles turned white, I raised my body to escape from this unknown feeling of having someone's mouth on my most scared part, he pushed my body on the bed holding it still. He raised his face to warn me with his eyes, I sight was so fucking sexy, his mouth was covered with my essence, he licked his lips and went back to the treasure that he found. He paid extra attention to my clit and sucked on the twins, I withered as I feel something building up in my lower

stomach
Unexpected something else joined his tongue I sucked in a huge breath at the intrusion. He slowly inserted his finger into my heat, the foreign feeling was uncomfortable until he curved his finger inside, that simple action hit something within me which had me coming undone calling out his name.
I slumped down on the bed as I came down from my first and most amazing orgasm ever. I know 26 and no masturbation what can I say I was shy and awkward
I glanced down to see Massimo slurping on the remains of my orgasm, it was the sexiest thing I have ever seen. His finger was still in me whereas his other hand joined my left breast squeezing and needing it.
He kissed my heat one last time before kissing me on my lips, my essence has a lingering taste in his mouth that turned me on even more. He realized my hair from the high pony and undid the braid, I was too high from my release that I didn't even feel him doing it.
He pressed his half-naked body on mine, his hard muscles and taut abs rubbed erotically on my soft skin. The hard tent in his pants was pressed against my lower part, and the feel of it was pretty big. I gulped nervously I can't even imagine how it actually looks.
As my lips were busy getting bruised my hands roamed on his sexy body, I circled his nips with both of my hands and he moaned in pleasure, he pulled his lips away from me and hid his face on my neck. His harsh breathing was turning me on to another extend.
My hands found their way towards hid pant buckle he held my wrist and looked into my eyes "you don't have to, " he said his chest heaving so was mine.

"I want to, " my liquor courage had already left my system this was completely me and this was something that I wanted to do.
He left my wrist and placed them on my breasts playing with them, I moaned in pleasure as my hands worked their way into his pants, his breath hitched as my hands moved into his boxers, I froze when my hand made contact with his crotch, it was smooth, hot and very hard. He grunted sexually, his responses were very encouraging.
I moved my hand on him before I could Chicken out and with every stroke, I felt bold enough to fasten my speed. He stopped me before I could go any further. "That's enough or I won't be able to control myself" he kissed my lips and pulled my hands out of his pants.
"Do you want to stop?" He asked but I knew he didn't want to stop and so did I.
"I want you, " my words brought a spark into his eyes, he pulled away from me and got rid of his pants and boxers, he was bigger than what I had felt and what worried me was how it's gonna fit? And how it's going to tear my insides out. He kissed my lips again, his tongue roamed around my mouth like he was looking for something or memorizing his way into it. His hands pulled and pinched on my nipples, his right hand moved between my legs and pushed them apart, he settled down between them, he wrapped my legs around his waist and pushed himself closer, so close that his crotch was not far from my heat. I placed my arms around his neck and concentrated on his lips as his fingers moved inside my heat, he stretched his way in adding another one I gasped with the intrusion, he curled his fingers hitting that amazing spot that had me curling my toes in the pleasure I felt another one of the orgasm building up ready to release

"I'm gonna... I'm gonna, " I couldn't even say the word but he seemed to understand my embarrassing
"Come for me, " he ordered, I did as he said and my body turned into mush with unbearable pleasure
I heaved looking at him as he watched me coming back from my high. He slowly pressed his thick hard penis into my heat, I moaned as my sensitive heat tingled with his warm meat.
"I won't be able to stop now," he said like a warning
I held his face in my palms and kissed his lips " I don't want you to, " my words boosted him to go on.
He slowly pressed his head into my heat, I gasped with the sensation and before I ask him to go on, he had pushed in all the way in. He swallowed my scream when he pressed his mouth on mine. Tears fell out of my eyes as he stayed still in his position.
He gave me a minute to get comfortable with him inside me. I whispered for him to move and he slowly moved inside me, pleasure replaced pain as he thrust forward. Every one of his thrusts was slow and it hit my bundle of nerves every time.
It wasn't long before he had me screaming his name as his pace increased, his hand pulled my hair and others held my neck almost choking, and unknown to me I actually love the way he handled my body, he Worshiped my body with love and kisses.
My toes stayed curled, my nails scratched his back with the intense pleasure I was feeling, I felt on top of the world, I met his thrusts with the same kind of intensity
"I'm not gonna last long, " he said moving eagerly inside me
"Me too, " and before we knew it, we released together.
Both of us breathing heavily, he kissed my lips sloppily,

before slumping down me, he pulled out making me hiss in pain, he kissed my forehead before apologizing, he moved away from me and I closed my eyes imaging him picking his clothes and leaving, tears slipped out of my eyes with those thoughts swirling in my head but something wet and cold touched my body

I opened my eyes to see him completely naked and wiping my body clean from the remains of our mess. I glanced at the little blood on it and grimaced, he smiled at my reaction and then back to the bathroom to throw the cloth. He came back to bed, covered us with the blanket, and pulled me closer to his body heat, I kissed him slowly amazed by his gentle behavior.

"I love you" he mumbled before closing his eyes, he instantly fell asleep, I smiled at his confession and kissed his forehead

"I love you too,"

I wake up feeling warm and fuzzy, I slowly open my eyes and watch my surroundings, frowning I try to recall the events of last night and was stunned, shocked, and amazed with myself.

I groan in the embarrassment of my boldness last night, I peek beside me and found, Massimo, sleeping soundly. I smiled at the peaceful look on his face and honestly, I don't regret last night, and I don't hate it too. Actually, last night was the most amazing night of my entire existence.

I peer down lifting the sheets on me and groan at the blood spot on the extremely white sheets. Slowly I move out of the bed trying to make the least noises and stared at my phone troubled with the time. Our flight to Greece, leaves within an hour and for the first time in my life I had to choose between Massimo and something else in my life, I showered quickly and changed into something nice which was difficult because there were hardly any clothes in the wardrobe for me, I left a small note for him saying I will be in Greece for Oliver and Pete's wedding, then ran to the airport like my ass was on fire.

"I know I'm late, " I meet up with Oliver and his friends at the airport lounge, my passport, and visa were already with me in my bag at the hotel room, I had to take a detour but luckily I was able to make it on time.

"I can see why" he teased pointing at his neck to gesture mine, I blush with the realization of where he was pointing at, there were many fading love bites marks all over my neck and body.

"Shut up, " he laughs, Nicole was already there enjoying her latte. We got on the plane and took off for the most beautiful city in the world.

When I was finally alone sitting next to a sleepy Nicole, I blushed at the memories of last night. I can't believe I finally did it, and I didn't regret it because it was with Massimo, I don't care if we have different paths in life he will always be an important part of my life

I woke up with a tap on my shoulder when it was time to land, we were finally in Greece, for the most important thing in Pete's life. The wedding was today at a local Church but the reception at this amazing beach, where the sand was white. I've read so much about this place I couldn't wait for it.

"Ready for the most stressful day of your life?" I teased Pete when we walked out of the airport, he glared at me playfully "Not helping, " I laugh at his nervousness, the limo was already here, we reached the hotel and didn't dwell into sightseeing, everything was already here except our clothes, which I remembered to get in a hurry. There were all men and no bride's maids which was fine because there was no bride, I was Pete's best girl so I dressed in a very beautiful and elegant baby pink long dress.

Oliver wore a traditional white three-piece suit, we reached the church at the noon, and the decor was just mind-blowing, everything was white flowers, tables, and venue. Everything is gorgeous in white.

Pete was standing beneath a large chandelier next to the priest, wearing matching suits smiling fondly when I walked Oliver down the aisle, he was trembling nervously, I held his arm tighter reassuringly, I was also holding a very large bouquet that had white lilies, I kissed his cheek and handed him over to an inpatient Pete

The ceremony was beautiful, all of their vows were self-written and I felt a stab in my chest when I recalled my wedding, there weren't even vows, but I was happy for him and wish him the best.

When the ceremony was over, we drove back to our hotel to get ready for the reception, we couldn't wait. The venue for the reception was just next door so, we didn't take the cars. I changed into a more comfortable short dress acceptable for the reception at the beach. We ate, met, and danced with various people

The first dance was obviously for the wedded grooms, the danced on the 'if our love is wrong' by Calum Scott from the album, 'only human ' I cried at that beautiful moment.

Now it was my turn for the speech, I stood on the sand with a microphone in my hand and a wine glass in other " I would like to raise a toast to the best brother-in-law in the whole wide world, Oliver Price-Miller, I never had a brother before but that was before I met Oliver, my first gay friend, and an honest companion. I wish you all the love, happiness, and lots and lots of babies, to Oliver and Pete, may the odds be in your favor" we laughed at the end of my speech

Oliver hugged thanking me, and Pete hugged me thanking me for being here for Oliver, we jumped into the sea when all the mushy stuff was over, I wore a blue bikini just sunbathing on the beach chairs. Finally the vacation I was praying for.

We spent the day at the beach drinking coconut water layered in sunscreen, it was finally time for sending the grooms off the do the naughty, but we stayed back at the beach, enjoying its nightlife. Nicole was flirting with a tourist that was throwing a party near our spot. We had fun for a while then minimum sleep took its toll on my body, I bid everyone good night and walked off towards my room.

When I unlocked the door and walked in, someone hit the back of my head with something heavy and I fell losing consciousness, and the last thing I remembered was a pair of leather shoes

A sharp pain shot through my head, a sense of Deja Vu flickered in my mind, I groan in pain on opening my eyes the bright lights Pierced through it blinding me momentarily.

I try to move my hand to shield my eyes but I couldn't, my hands were bound, I looked at myself and I found myself bound with ropes on a wooden chair, my lips sealed with the tape I observe my surroundings and I was trapped in some kind of a warehouse.

I tried to scream but no use, my voice was muffled by the tape. I tried to move but all my attempts to escape failed.

The door of the warehouse opened and I was shocked to see Oliver's Father, I felt betrayed because I had considered Oliver my brother, I try to console myself that maybe it's some misunderstanding and Oliver didn't betray me.
He slowly walked towards me and smirked his wrinkled face turned into an ugly look. " got something to say, Princess?" He mocked me
I glared at him and he laughed "oh, she's wild I like wild, " he said lustfully, I grimaced at him
"Arthur, that's enough," said a familiar voice, the blood drained from my face when the new face walked into the room. "Nice to see you again, Erika, " he smiled creepily, I stared at him terrified I can't believe it's him "please, take off the duck tape Artur, I'm sure she has a few questions for us, " he didn't even have to raise his voice for Artur to follow his order.
The duck tape ripped from my lips, I hissed at the pain, and Artur smiled giddy, I turned my attention to the newcomer and he was right I have didn't a lot of questions. "Why am I here, Robert, " yes Rober as in my Grandfather-in-law.
He smiled "it's very simple my dear, he took something important from me and I took something from him, " he hinted, I staggered in my seat with the realization
"So, that's it. Do you want revenge? I look at him bewildered " well sorry to tell you this but you got the wrong person, we don't even like each other. Our marriage was a contract" the moment the words left my mouth my captures gape at one another, "God, you did all of this for nothing, I feel bad for you, " I chuckled angrily. I knew I was babbling to distract them. On the other hand, I was twirling my finger ring because my ring was no ordinary ring there was a tracking chip, I have updated all of my devices for times like

these, and the alert goes to my friend Luke the Hacker, there were zero chances he would miss this.
They leave hurriedly not before slapping my face, my face spanned on the right side and I felt numb on my left cheek, I licked my lip and tasted blood within no time the cheek would be swollen too. I distract myself by working on my ring, there was a vibration and it was a sign that he got my message.
A few minutes later, both of them came back to the room looking smug, Robert stood in front of me, Artur walked behind me and pulled my hair, I winced in pain when the pain doubles with the previous hit.
"Looks like you were wrong, he does care about you, " Robert says showing me a video of Massimo entering some kind of dock.
"Why are you doing this, Robert, I know it isn't just about the Price property, moreover he is still your grandson, " I try to reason with him and he scoffs, and Arthur's grip tightens on my hair.
"You and I both know he isn't my grandson, but this doesn't concern you because when he gets here both of you will be dead, " he smirks evil before I could ask anything else they tape my mouth and leave, I just pray that Massimo has enough backup because shit is getting real tonight
I don't know how long it had been because slowly I was losing consciousness, there were loud noises outside the warehouse and I hoped it was Robert and his men that we're getting their ass kicked
But my prayers when unanswered because when the voices stopped there were gunshots, like a lot and a lot of gunfire. When the door opened my hopes turned and slapped me on my face because they dragged in a bloody, Massimo inside

the old cabin. I screamed and moved around on the chair but the ropes dug deeper into my skin. Massimo glanced at me his eyes bloody

"Erika, " he smiled exhausted I yell for him to keep his eyes open but I bloody tape blocked. Robert ripped the tape off of me and I bit his hand harshly, he backhands me the taste of copper filled my mouth. Massimo lunged at Robert but one of the guards kicked him down and kept kicking him until he could move again

"Stop, please stop, " I plead tearing up

"So much for hate huh, " Robert mocked I glared at him

"Stop it, Robert, he is still your grandson you raised him, " I scream but a punch in my stomach, got me screaming out in pain.

"He is not my grandson, I don't know how this fucker survived and switched himself with my grandson, now I will finish what my son had started, " he announced pulling out his gun aiming at Massimo's head.

"Stop, Robert, let's talk this through" I plead him if I know luke he might have already arranged someone to rescue me.

"Ok, anyway, both of you are going to die. how about I tell you everything, I mean you deserve to know why you have to die, Erika, " he smiled at me with a crazed look on his face. " there was a time when the Price, the family was considered the second most dangerous family in the mafia business, " I look at him wide eyes on the mention of Mafia businesses. " for generations there was one family that was always the first one, the Torricelli family, " he looks at Massimo in hatred

Massimo grinned proudly at Robert's hateful expression " they had to be stopped and lucky for us there was only one successor, with a family of his own but the heir was too

young to take over, that when we planned out to finish them off once and for all. My son attacked them at night and tortured them right in front of their heir, did you know he also had a little sister?" Robert smirks when Massimo snarred at him angrily,
"Poor child, she was only four, " he mocked Massimo, and Artur snickered amused "but my idiot of a son didn't check everyone were really dead, a few weeks later when my son and his family were traveling back they had an 'accident ' and every one of them died, " he paused clenching his fists
"My son and I weren't on talking terms back then so I didn't know how old his son was and accepted this scoundrel as my grandson and raised him, how I didn't realize that I was raising a snake, " he enraged
Massimo chuckled "you were so desperate by your guilt, poor grandpa didn't even notice there was no resemblance between me and his son, " he earned a kick in the gut
The situation was getting worst by the second and I could only pray that Luke would hurry and rescue me before Robert killed us both

The storytime was over when Robert looked at us seriously and we were running out of time as Robert and his goons pulled out their guns aiming at our heads. I keep twirling my ring restlessly. Just when he was about to press on the trigger, the gun was shot out of his hand.
Everyone in the room stayed on high alert when one by one everyone was shot down, I looked at Massimo he nodded at me and jumped on the guy near him and pulled out his gun, shot him dead, there were only four of us left, there seems to be a sniper that shot four guys down. Massimo shot Arthur's leg and he fell screaming in pain, Massimo aimed

his gun at Robert hesitant to pull the trigger.
"It's over Robert, this stops today" Robert scoffed angrily and reached for his gun but Massimo shot his leg as well the older guy fell groaning in pain, he ran towards me and undid my ropes. I hugged him crying when I was free, he held me tighter
I pulled away from him and he wiped tears, he noticed the swollen cheek and torn lip, his eyes darkened "who?" He asked scarily, I shook my head
"It doesn't matter, it's over now, " I say pulling away from him, a groan of pain caught my attention and I walked towards Artur he looked at me, I smiled at him sarcastically before kicking him in the face breaking his nose, I turned to face Massimo and he looked at me amused
The door burst open, cops flooded in screaming in, we smiled at each other and he hugged me closer when they got us out of there. They arrested Robert and Artur for kidnapping and attempt to murder charges.
Oliver hugged me weeping and apologizing nonstop for what his father did, I reassured him that he shouldn't apologize for something that he didn't do.
I had a dislocated wrist, swollen face, and bruised ego whereas Massimo had gunshot wounds and broken ribs. I stayed in his hospital room, he was unconscious and hasn't woken up from the surgery.
I held his hand in mine and waited for him to wake up. I laid my head on his bed crying silently if things didn't work out I would have lost him again and this time it would have stayed like that.
"Stop crying, Erika, I'm right here, " my head snapped towards him and I lunged at him, he winced when my hand made contact with his ribs. I apologize for that and kissed

his lips deeply proving that he is really alright.
"I won't be able to do anything if you keep kissing me like that, " he laughed and then flinched in pain.
I hit his shoulder and hugged him carefully trying not to hurt him. He kissed my forehead lovingly "I'm here Erika, I promise I will always be here, " I cried on his shoulder holding him closer
We stayed like that for a while, "Erika, do me a favor and get my jacket, " I nodded walking towards the couch retrieving his jacket I held it out for him to take "open the right pocket and take out my watch, " he said, I frowned searching his jacket pocket but there was no phone "empty it, " I scowl at him for troubling so much, I carefully pulled out the pocket and something fell out
I bend over to pick up the small thing but froze when I saw what it was. I picked it up and showed it to him, he smiled at me sheepishly "I would go down on my knees, but I can't right now and I don't want to wait any longer, " I squeaked excitedly and jumped on him hugging him tightly "gentle, gently" he laughed painfully.
I kissed every corner of his face " I don't know what to say, " I say emotionally,
"Don't, because I have something to ask you, " he said pushing the hair out of my face, "Erika Black, will you please make me the happiest man on earth and marry me, again?"
I laughed at his proposal and nodded kissing his lips, he put the diamond ring on my ring finger and kissed my lips tenderly
A few months later
"My commitment to you is one if give willingly, absolutely, and without hesitation. I am yours utterly and have been since the moment we met. We were married before this day

and will always be." Massimo vowed with a loving look in his eyes

The priest looked at me and I smiled gazing at the love of my life

"When I hold your face in my hands or lean into your shoulder to feel you hold me, I know this is the place I am meant to be for all time. This is the person with whom I am meant to share my life." I vow to smile brightly

"Do you Massimo Torricelli, take Erika Black as your lawfully wedded wife in sickness and health, to love and cherish her till the end of the day, promise to support her in every step of life?" The priest asked him, Massimo's eyes didn't longer away he smiled at me "I do, "

"Do you Erika black take This man Massimo Torricelli as your lawfully wedded husband in sickness and health, to love and cherish him till the end of the day, promise to support him in every step of life?" The Priest asked me smiling encouragingly

I smiled at Massimo "I do, "

"You may now kiss the bride, " Massimo pulled me closer by the waist, kissing my lips gently. We kissed passionately until the Priest cleared his throat to get our attention

I look at the crowd and find all of my friends and family, my mother crying happy tears, Oliver jumping in his place excitedly, my sister and her husband smiling holding their five-year-old son. Nicole was grinning every single person looked at us and I looked at my husband and smiled, I'm happy for us too because all of my wishes come true.

www.ingramcontent.com/pod-product-compliance
Lightning Source LLC
La Vergne TN
LVHW100334181026
850499LV00039B/1067
* 9 7 8 9 3 5 4 5 8 2 3 2 5 *